SOFIE'S BOYS

JENIKA SNOW

SOFIE'S BOYS

By Jenika Snow

www.JenikaSnow.com

Jenika_Snow@Yahoo.com

Copyright © July 2019 by Jenika Snow

First ebook publication © July 2019 Jenika Snow

Photographer: Wander Aguiar Photography

Cover Model: Jonny James & Wander Aguiar

Image provided by: Wander Book Club

Cover design by: Designs by Dana

Editor: Kasi Alexander

Content Editor: Kayla Robichaux

Proofreader: Read by Rose

ALL RIGHTS RESERVED: The unauthorized reproduction, transmission, or distribution of any part of this copyrighted work is illegal. Criminal copyright infringement is investigated by the FBI and is punishable by up to five years in federal prison and a fine of $250,000.

This literary work is fiction. Any name, places, characters and incidents are the product of the author's imagination. Any resemblance to actual persons, living or dead, events or establishments is solely coincidental.

Please respect the author and do not participate in or encourage piracy of copyrighted materials that would violate the author's rights.

I fell in love with two men. I thought being with them both—at the same time—would be complicated.

But it was easy. It was perfect.

One of them was twice my age.

The other was the boy I'd grown up with.

Both of them were so very different, but they gave me exactly what I wanted, exactly what I needed.

Ryker was a bad boy with looks that had my panties dropping from day one. He knew exactly where to touch me to make me cry out for more.

He was also my best friend.

Jareth was older, refined, and experienced. He knew how to make me beg for more with just a dominant look.

He was also my boss.

Although they were possessive and jealous where I was concerned, they accepted I was in a relationship with both of them.

Ryker and Jareth only demanded one thing from me—to only be with them.

But would I have choose to be with just one?

How wrong would it be if I kept them both?

CHAPTER ONE

Sofie

I thought it would be complicated being in a relationship with two men at the same time.

But it wasn't. It was easy.

They were so different from each other, yet gave me exactly what I needed.

Ryker was the typical bad boy with the leather-jacket-wearing, Harley-riding, MC vibe going on.

My best friend, the one person I'd grown up with, and the boy I'd given my virginity to.

And then there was Jareth. Older and sophisticated, he controlled the boardroom like it was his bitch.

He was also my boss. He dominated me in ways I never imagined, never even thought I'd enjoy.

Here I was, seeing them both, in a relationship with two men. And to be honest, I didn't know how it all started, how I'd gotten in a situation in which I was in love with two separate people, almost as if I were living two very different lives.

Sure, I'd been called a slut by some when they found out I was with two men, but Ryker and Jareth were two who equaled one.

One perfect man for me.

Jareth's dominance was cold and hard, like polished steel moving over my body as I let it cool over.

Ryker's familiarity was like smooth wood warmed by the sun as I lay on it and basked in the heat.

Jareth fucked.

Ryker made love.

But then again, they'd been known to switch it up on me, to show me sides of themselves I'd never experienced, never thought they were capable of.

They were mine and I was theirs.

Always.

I ran the lipstick over my bottom lip, put the cap back on, and looked at myself in the mirror.

Tonight was Ryker's night, and although I'd known him my entire life, our relationship had drastically changed once things became sexual, once we went from being just friends to... something more.

It had all changed with that first kiss, that first touch, then the heated moment of me begging Ryker to take my virginity. Booze had been involved—of course. The party we'd attended was wild and sexually charged, which then led to us in the back of his pickup with him on top of me.

Jareth, on the other hand... well, I blamed that on the animal magnetism that poured off him in waves, and a company Christmas party where I drank too much champagne. Because that had ended with me in Jareth's office with his face between my thighs.

And then came the day when they both came to me and wanted more, wanted a relationship. Although there had only been that one time I'd been with each of them, I'd grown feelings for them, and knew choosing one over the other was an impossible task.

So I'd told both of them about the other, explained I couldn't let either of them go, that I cared too much about them both. I'd expected them to end it with me right then and there. But surprisingly they'd agreed, told me almost identically that they refused to give me up, that if they had to share me with the other, so be it.

They were possessive and territorial of me when it concerned other men, but with each other? They were accepting, conceding that I couldn't give them up.

So here I was, living two separate lives, having two separate relationships, and in love with both Ryker and Jareth.

"What a story," I said to my reflection.

I finished getting ready, my belly tightening with each passing second. I'd been seeing both Jareth and Ryker for months now, and every day I felt my feelings for them grow. I loved them. And although I knew they cared about me too, there was this little voice in the back of my head that reminded me this could all end horribly.

Maybe this wasn't real. I mean, it sure sounded fictional. Me with two men, both of them desperate for my attention, possessive of me....

If I was being honest, it all sounded too good to be true.

But everything had been going so smoothly, so perfectly. Once things had become official between

Ryker and Jareth, it had all fallen into place perfectly, as if that's how it was always meant to be.

I split my days up every week between them. Three days on, three days off, and one day I had for myself. Although, if I were being truthful, if I could spend every single day of every single week with both of them, it would be nirvana.

I gave myself one last long look in the mirror before heading downstairs. My roommate was sitting on the couch, a pint of ice cream in her lap, and *When Harry Met Sally* playing on the TV for the hundredth time.

I grabbed my purse and checked to make sure I had all the essentials: lipstick, deodorant, gum, and my wallet.

I heard the loud rumble of a motorcycle approaching, and my pulse raced, butterflies moving wildly inside me. I walked to the window, pulling the curtain aside and seeing Ryker come to a stop in the driveway.

"I always know when you're about to leave, because I can hear his motorcycle or see the fancy Mercedes pulling up in the driveway," Kati shouted from the living room and then promptly looked over her shoulder and grinned.

She liked to tease me about how she was jealous,

how she couldn't believe I was in a relationship with two men and they were totally okay with it.

I'd always just say, *"You and me both."* Because I couldn't believe it either.

"Don't wait up," I said as I opened the door, not giving Ryker the chance to come get me.

This was his third night, meaning it was the last night I'd see him until next week. But that was the agreement we'd all come up with, and it had been working seamlessly so far.

Although I hated going these long stretches without seeing him or Jareth, I couldn't lie and say that having some time apart was also nice, almost liberating. It gave everyone time to themselves.

I shut the front door behind me and rounded the corner, seeing Ryker dismount, a helmet under his arm and his focus on me. He didn't grin, didn't show any kind of expression, but that was usual. He was the strong, silent type, brooding and intense, serious but with a playful side.

And that playful side just happened to be when we were in his bed, both of us naked, his big body on top of mine as he commanded me like he knew me inside and out.

I guess that was the similarity between Jareth and Ryker. They were both so intense, so serious all the time. But they showed me a gentle side, one that was sweet and endearing but also told me—showed me and taught me—who was really in control.

I might have had power over them both, but they wielded something far stronger within me.

Desire. Love.

When I was within reaching distance, he set the helmet down and reached out for me, curled his fingers around my hip, and pulled me against his hard body. I melted against him, slowly trailing my gaze up his body so I could look into his face.

He was six-foot four inches of pure, unadulterated masculinity, with his arms and chest covered in tattoos, the description "tall, dark, and handsome" fitting him perfectly. He was brutal, was completely devoted to me, and was what I would consider an all-around male.

And he was mine.

He stared into my eyes, this possessive expression on his face. He made a deep sound in his throat before he slid his hand up to cup my cheek, and then he leaned down and kissed me. His lips on mine were owning, consuming.

He slid his tongue along the seam of my mouth, urging me to open without saying anything. I felt the hard evidence of his arousal pressing against my belly, and I rose on my toes and wrapped my arms around his neck, keeping him close as he mouth-fucked me.

There was no other phrase to describe what he was doing.

In and out, he thrust his tongue in my mouth, stroking it with mine, pulling a soft moan from me as I felt arousal move through my body. My panties instantly became wet, my nipples hardening. But he pulled away before things got too heated, before he fucked me against the side of the garage. Which I knew he would, and I was tempted to beg him to do just that.

He made a deep rumble that came from his chest, his hand still cupping my cheek, his focus on me.

"Why'd you stop?" I whispered those words and tried to kiss him again, but the small smirk that played across his lips had me groaning in frustration and pulling back.

Although Ryker wasn't a dominating lover, not like Jareth, he did hold a lot of sexual power over me, liked to play with the desire, withhold it, and make me beg for it.

And God, did I beg for it.

"I want to wine and dine my girl tonight." He had

his hand on the small of my back and slid it down to cup my ass. He curled those digits around one of the globes, his fingers perilously close to the crease, the tips only needing a few more inches before he'd be touching between my thighs.

If I just shifted a little bit, I bet he'd be touching my pussy right now. I thought about doing it, act like it was an accident, even if we both knew that was bullshit. But before I could act on that, he pulled his hand away. He gave my ass one hard swat and leaned down to claim my mouth.

When he pulled back, he reached for the helmet he'd set on the seat and handed it to me to put on.

Once it was on, I straddled the bike, a little bit disappointed I'd been forced to wear jeans.

They didn't give easy access, and when I was with Ryker, my thoughts were dirty.

He climbed on, looked over his shoulder before starting the engine, and asked where I wanted to eat.

I had my arms wrapped around his waist, the hardness of his muscles instantly causing this feminine sigh to leave me.

"Anywhere as long as you're there," I said. Hey, it was corny, I admit, but I'd known Ryker nearly my entire life. We started off as playmates, then friends, and now were in the next stage as lovers. I loved him so much, and although I was cheesy at times, I knew secretly he liked that, even with his bad-boy, Harley-riding persona.

He still looked at me over his shoulder, but his expression remained stoic. He leaned in slightly and kissed me, and I met him halfway, our lips pressing gently together, another sigh leaving me.

He backed out of the driveway and we headed to wherever he wanted. I wasn't picky. In fact, I didn't even care if we went to dinner. I'd much rather just spend the rest of the evening naked and in his bed, his arms around me as he fucked me.

But when he pulled into the parking lot of this little bistro restaurant he knew I loved, I held in my disappointment at not heading straight to his place.

Once we dismounted and went inside, we were taken to a table almost immediately. We got some glasses of water, ordered a bottle of wine, and started looking over the menu. I glanced up from mine to stare at him. He was so big and intimidating looking, and to strangers he was pretty aloof, maybe almost frightening in appearance. But if they really knew Ryker, they'd see he was a big teddy bear. Or maybe that was just with me.

I felt myself smile at that thought.

Once we placed our order, I asked Ryker how his

day had gone. Not only did he have a business degree, but he also owned his own motorcycle repair shop. He was smart and talented, and God... did he know how to work with his hands.

I cleared my throat. "So, Ryker." I watched as he set the menu on the table. The look he gave me told me that he knew whatever I was about to ask was probably typical Sofie. Which meant it was pointless, cheesy, or full-on dirty.

"So, Sofie," he rumbled in his deeply masculine voice.

"I have a question for you."

He grinned. "Should I be nervous?"

I chuckled softly and shook my head. "No. I'm just curious is all. I've actually been wondering this for a while, but I guess I didn't want to stick my nose where it didn't belong."

"But now you want to stick your nose where it doesn't belong?" He smirked again.

"Well, you know me." I shrugged and returned the smile.

"Okay," he said and leaned back in the chair, the chatter of the patrons around us enjoying their meal fading away as I stared into his dark eyes.

God, I could get lost in those eyes. "After we, you know, for the first time..." I looked around to make sure no one could hear me. I didn't know why I was bringing this up now. It's not like it mattered in the grand scheme of things. But it was something I'd wondered.

"After we fucked for the first time in the back of my truck?"

I felt my face heat at his blunt words. Leave it to Ryker to say it like it was.

He leaned forward and gave me a sexy grin. "Yeah, I think about that moment every time I jerk off, Sofie."

Oh. God.

I was tempted to say screw the question and dinner and go back to his place.

The waitress came and refilled our drinks, and I was thankful for the small reprieve to gather myself.

Once she left, I cleared my throat. "After that, since we weren't like together-together..." He lifted his eyebrow. and I stopped talking for a second. "You know, like in a relationship or anything. Did you see anyone?"

"See anyone?" He still had a dark eyebrow lifted, a stoic expression on his face.

I shrugged, feeling all kinds of awkward even bringing this up, to even care, given the fact I was seeing Jareth as well.

"You mean did I fuck anyone else after we did?"

Once again, my cheeks heated. I nodded and glanced around. But no one cared about us or what we spoke about.

He didn't speak for long moments, and I diverted my gaze because of my embarrassment. I looked at him then, watched as he leaned forward and braced his forearms on the table, his focus trained solely on me. "No, Sofie. I wasn't fucking anyone else. I wasn't even dating anyone for that matter." He kept his expression void.

I was surprised by that. "Really? Can I ask why?" It wasn't any of my damn business, but the words spilled from me before I could stop them.

It was silent for a long moment, and he leaned back in the chair once more, looking at me as if he had questions of his own. "Honestly?"

I nodded. "Always. You know that."

"Because you're all I wanted. You're all I've ever wanted."

The world faded from me after he spoke.

"Did I have offers?" He nodded. "Yeah. A lot. But no one else holds a candle to you, Sof."

I felt all kinds of things in that moment.

"Did you fuck anyone else after us, aside from what's his name?" The corner of his mouth kicked up in a smirk, but I could tell he was anything but amused.

Although Jareth and Ryker tolerated the fact I was with both of them, they were insanely possessive of me.

I shook my head. "No, I wasn't with anyone, not until Jareth, and even then I hadn't planned it or anything."

One rule was we never spoke about the other while together. Same went when I was with Jareth. But there were those times things like this came up. And when they did, we worked—and talked—through them like adults.

"It just happened." He didn't say that to be condescending. He said it as if he understood.

I swallowed the thick lump in my throat, the conversation turning extremely serious, even though that hadn't been my intention. We didn't speak for long moments, those words hanging between us.

"Listen, this got too heavy for how I planned on this night going," he said in his deep voice. "Now that it's out of the way, let's finish eating." He leaned in again. "Unless you wanna skip dinner and go right to dessert?"

And just like that, I was flushed, aroused, and the topic of fucking other people was a distant memory.

CHAPTER TWO

Sofie

We found ourselves back at Ryker's place. It was a small two-bedroom house, the typical bachelor pad one might expect.

When he first showed me this place, I couldn't understand what the appeal was. That was until we went to the back and there was a massive garage sitting on almost two acres of land.

Then it all made sense.

Ryker was the type of guy who worked with his hands, did grungy, backbreaking manual labor, because he enjoyed it. Not only did he work on cars and motorcycles as his job, but he also did it during his free time, because he genuinely enjoyed it.

"Beer?" he asked as we stepped through the front door. He tossed his keys onto the small dining room table and walked into the kitchen.

Although we'd ordered a bottle of wine at dinner, he'd only had one glass with his meal, and I'd finished off the rest. I had a nice buzz going on, but I still nodded. I wasn't the biggest beer drinker, but Ryker always had the best craft ones on hand.

I went over to the living room and sat in his oversized recliner. Although it would comfortably fit two people, because Ryker was such a big guy, he filled up the entire thing. The leather was soft like butter beneath me, and smelled just like him.

I heard the fridge open and close, the sound of beer bottles clanking together, and then a moment later I sensed him walking into the living room.

Looking over my shoulder, I appreciated the sight that was all him.

He set the bottles on the coffee table, looking at me hungrily. Although we did things as a couple, almost mundane experiences that you'd expect a boyfriend and girlfriend to do, we were also both extremely passionate. That meant when we were alone, giving each other pleasure was at the top of our list.

I was about to push myself up to stand, propel this evening along, but he was in front of me a moment later, dropping to his knees and sliding his hands up my thighs. He kept his focus trained right on my eyes as he unbuttoned my jeans and pulled the zipper down. He curled his fingers around the waistband, taking my jeans and my panties down with them.

A soft moan left me.

I lifted my ass to give him better access, and once the clothes were off and tossed to the side, he leaned back so he was sitting on his heels. Ryker slowly trailed his gaze down to my pussy. Although my legs were closed, I had no doubt he could see my slit.

He wrapped his hand loosely around my leg and lifted my foot, putting it on his shoulder and then leaning in and running his tongue around the delicate bone of my ankle. He kissed and sucked at my skin, moving his tongue and lips up my calf then closer to my inner thigh. With his free hand, he lifted my other leg and placed it over the arm of the chair.

I felt myself spread for him, felt the cool air move along the most intimate part of my body.

I had my hands wrapped around the leather, my nails digging in as pleasure instantly consumed me and he'd hardly even touched me yet. He wrapped his hands around my waist and pulled me down lower so my ass was hanging off the seat of the chair. And then he took my foot off his shoulder and put my leg over the other armrest.

I was obscenely spread for him, my stomach hollowing in and out, in and out. I exhaled harshly, the pleasure taking over. He kept his face expressionless, but it still spoke volumes.

He was hungry for me. He'd devour me.

"I don't know if I can last until I see you again, baby." He grunted out those words and leaned in closer, his eyes trained on mine. "If I'm being honest, those days I don't see you, I jerk off so many times that my dick gets sore."

A small sound left me, and I felt my nipples harden.

He looked down at my pussy, a low growl leaving him. "Look at how wet you are for me." Ryker slid his hand along my inner thigh, moved it closer to the spot between my legs, and then he was sliding his fingers up and down my slit, gathering my arousal. "Soaked." He grunted that lone word right before he leaned in to latch his mouth right on my center.

I closed my eyes and tipped my head back, my mouth opening on its own as I moaned softly. The feel of him flattening his tongue and sliding it up and down my cleft, dipping it into my pussy hole, and then dragging it back up and sucking on my nub was almost my undoing.

"Look at me," he demanded, the vibrations from his voice spearing right through my core.

I forced myself to lift my head, to open my eyes. I stared at him, seeing this almost animalistic look on his face. That's the most accurate description I could come up with for how he watched me.

He pulled back just enough so that he could see my pussy, so that I could see how wet I was. And then he stuck his tongue out and flattened it on me once more. He dragged it up and down again, lapping at my clit and moving the muscle around the hardened, engorged bud. He growled deeply, as if he were in heaven right now.

I gasped at the sensitivity.

He had his thumbs on either side of my lips, pulling the flesh apart, spreading me out for him. He moved his tongue back down and thrust it into my hole, fucking me there like I wanted him to do with his big cock.

"Please, Ryker." I licked my lips, my voice no

more than a whisper. He growled low before giving my pussy one last suck, and then he leaned back.

We stared at each other for a prolonged moment, the electricity and chemistry bouncing between us.

With his hands back on my inner thighs, keeping me spread, I was at his mercy.

"What do you want?" His voice was a rough tenor, sounding slightly husky, very serrated.

"I want you," I said honestly, because there was no point in sugarcoating all of this. I was here, spread for him, all but begging to be fucked. I wanted him desperately, and I knew he wanted me too.

He let go of me and stood, and I watched with a no doubt heated gaze as he went for the button and zipper of his jeans. But he didn't take his pants fully off, and instead pulled his cock out of the fly, stroking himself from root to crown over and over again, pre-cum lining the tip.

He looked between my legs the entire time.

"Fuck me," I pleaded.

He didn't give me what I wanted though. As he still stared at my pussy while he masturbated, I knew he'd withhold from me. He liked that, loved having it build. This was about prolonging it, making me wait until I saw him the next time. And

God, did that anticipation feel so good when we finally came together.

"Touch your pretty cunt for me," he ordered. "Make yourself come for me."

I didn't hesitate as I reached down and ran my fingers through my cleft. I was soaking wet, my inner muscles clenching rhythmically as if they wanted something thick and long shoved deep inside of me. I moved my fingers up to my clit and framed the little bundle of nerves, moving the digits around it, feeling that pleasure climb higher and higher. And still, Ryker just stood there, moving his palm over the shaft, his gaze bouncing between my pussy and my face, back down to between my legs, and then looking back in my eyes.

He was breathing harder, heavier, his broad chest rising and falling. I knew he was close to getting off, knew he was forcing himself to hold off until I came.

I slipped my finger down and teased my pussy hole right before I shoved the digit inside. I thrust my breasts out and gasped, the sensation so pronounced I couldn't keep the sound to myself.

"That's it, Sofie. Fuck yourself."

I opened my mouth on a silent sound as I did just that, pushing my finger in and out of my body, feeling my muscles pulling at the digit, trying to draw it in farther. I watched as he stroked himself, stared at the pre-cum that lined the hole at the tip. There was so much of it, the clear fluid dripping from the crown. He was so worked up for me—that was evident.

He ran his palm over the tip of his dick, gathering the pre-cum and using it as lubrication. And as we touched ourselves in front of each other, I found that completion almost instantly. All I could do was close my eyes and tilt my head back, crying out as the orgasm finally claimed me.

I was vaguely aware of him grunting, felt his body heat as he moved closer. I opened my eyes and looked at him, saw he was standing between my legs now, still working himself over, but clearly very close to getting off.

"Come on, Ryker," I said in a sultry voice. I saw his neck muscles strain, knew he was close because of the fierce look on his face. A second later, he came.

He let out a deep rumble as jet after jet of milky white semen shot out in arcs from his cock and landed between my legs. Fluid covered my pussy, painting it, proving he'd been just as worked up as I was. Despite the fact we'd had sex several times in our three days together, his load was massive, so much cum that I didn't stop myself from reaching down and rubbing it all over my cunt.

I smoothed it in like it was lotion, needing his scent covering me.

"That's it. Fucking rub my cum into your skin."

I continued to do just that, my mouth slightly open as I panted, aftershocks of pleasure moving through me.

When both of us were spent, he tucked himself back in his jeans and helped me to stand. Ryker pulled me in close, my pants and panties still off, his hands now cupping my ass. He squeezed the mounds until I was rising on my toes to get closer to him.

"Mine, Sofie. You're fucking mine and I love you." He slid his hand up my back and cupped my nape. He leaned in and claimed my mouth, making me taste myself on his lips and tongue.

He made me take his kiss.

And I did, because when it came to Ryker, I was helpless to do anything else.

CHAPTER THREE

Sofie

I carried in the two cups of coffee, my bag slung over my shoulder, and my heels clicking on the marble floor. I tried to look at my watch to see how late it actually was, happened to get a glance, and internally cursed as I picked up my speed.

Although I was sleeping with the boss, in a serious relationship with him, that didn't mean I could be late whenever the hell I felt like it. But thanks to my alarm not going off, coupled with city traffic, I was hauling ass this morning.

I pushed the button to go up on the elevator then stood there as I waited for the doors to open. I replayed the last three days in my head, still tingling all over from Ryker. Although we hadn't slept together last night, not in a sexual sense, we'd gotten in his bed and just lay there. He'd kept his arms around me, the conversation easy and relaxed. I'd forced myself to leave at a decent time, knowing I had to get up for work, but here I was, still late.

I should have just slept over.

But I also couldn't lie and say I wasn't insanely excited to see Jareth. Even though he was my employer, I didn't actually see him during work hours. It was a rare occasion when our paths crossed at the office, and when they did, we always kept it professional. Hell, no one at work even knew I was with him. That's how discreet and professional we kept that shit.

So it wasn't technically "breaking the rules" when it was Ryker's three days and I was at work with Jareth.

But today was the start of Jareth's three days, and that meant after work I'd head straight to his place, stay with him for the next seventy-two hours, and then leave and have the next day to myself.

This V relationship was like a well-oiled machine, where I was at the point, and Jareth and Ryker were split off from me but still connected.

Once I was at work, I smiled as I passed cubicles and headed toward my office. Although I had my own space, it wasn't anything grand, nothing like an executive or even a junior executive suite. But it worked for me, gave me privacy to get work done, and if I wanted to get crazy during Jareth's time, I'd email him some extremely inappropriate and not-safe-for-work messages.

I set a coffee down on my assistant's desk, and she mouthed a thank you as she held the phone to her ear.

"Just give me the day's rundown when you're done," I whispered, and she nodded.

I took my coffee and headed into my office, closing the door with the heel of my shoe and walking to my desk. I tossed my bag on the table, went around to sit down, and booted up my computer. As I waited for it to warm up, I looked out my window while I sipped from my paper cup, the vanilla chai latte almost too hot to drink.

I was lost in thought when I heard the ding that told me I had a new message. Focusing on the computer, I moved the mouse around until I could click on the little icon that had an envelope with a red 1 hovering above it.

I opened up my email and immediately felt my

belly tighten in excitement. It was from Jareth. My throat went dry as I thought about what he had written to me. I didn't even have to see him for my body to light up, for arousal to lick across my skin and settle deep within my core.

To: **Sofie Blackwell (Stein Enterprise, Assistant Media Director)**

From: **Jareth Stein (Stein Enterprise, CEO)**

Miss Blackwell, it's come to my attention that you're twenty minutes late. I'll need to see you in my office during your lunch hour, to go over the employee handbook and the rules of conduct.

Although his email sounded foreboding, even reprimanding, I knew it wasn't anything but sexual. It had nothing to do with punishing me, and everything to do with an excuse for him to see me. And he certainly wasn't wasting any time on his first day.

I set my coffee down and placed my hands on the keyboard to type out the reply.

To: Jareth Stein (Stein Enterprise, CEO)

From: Sofie Blackwell (Stein Enterprises, Assistant Media Director)

Dear Mr. Stein. My apologies for not being professional and being to work on time. I'll be in your office promptly at noon to go over the employee handbook so I'm updated and versed on what's expected of me.

My body positively tingled at the very thought of what we'd do in his office, how exactly he'd put me "in my place." Now I just had to go about the rest of the day, or at least until lunchtime, trying not to let the dirty images of Jareth and me together consume my thoughts.

———

I stood on the other side of Jareth's office door, the mahogany smooth, the grain dark. Everyone had gone to lunch, including his personal assistant, and even though this wasn't a new relationship, I felt the tendrils of those butterflies moving in my stomach, the nervousness that came with the first date settling in my body. I lifted my hand and brought my knuckles down on the wood, three sharp raps that sounded dense.

"Come in, Sofie."

I could hear the deep tenor of his voice, and it slammed right into my center. The command would've had my toes curling if not for the stiletto heels I wore—the kind Jareth loved.

I blew out a slow breath, gripped the cold, brass handle, and opened the door. He stood by his floor-to-ceiling window, overlooking the city, his hands shoved in the pockets of his slacks, his broad shoulders seeming to take up my entire view.

"Close the door behind you," he said in a calm, even voice, but there was a hint of authority laced with it. He turned and watched me, saying nothing else as he stared at me for long moments. I always felt like I was under a microscope when I was around him, his gaze so penetrating it was almost... intimate.

My feelings for him were different than what I felt for Ryker. Although I loved them equally, desired them so passionately I couldn't even breathe at times, Jareth was a dominating lover. He liked to control in the bedroom, to control every aspect of his life.

Ryker, on the other hand, was focused on making me get off, as if he needed it before he could find his own release.

Jareth withheld my pleasure, because it got *him* off.

Maybe that's why I'd fallen in love with them both. Maybe having two very different men who catered to my twin desires, my dual needs, was what I needed to feel complete.

"Come here, Sofie."

I smoothed my hands down my pencil skirt and started making my way toward him. When I got to his desk, I stopped. And then I just breathed out slowly as I waited for him to make a move, to make a command.

It got me off when he told me what to do, because although it might seem like he held the power, the truth was I held it all.

"You were really late this morning," he said matter-of-factly.

I really wasn't, just twenty minutes or so, but I didn't correct him. I didn't dare. Instead, I nodded and clasped my hands behind my back in a purely submissive move.

"Why were you late?" He took a step forward, his hands still in the pockets of his slacks, his focus trained on me.

Jareth was older than me, twenty years to be exact. At twenty-four, I'd never thought I'd fall in love with a man my father's age. Hell, I didn't think I could fall in love with *two* men at the same time either. Funny how life worked.

"My alarm didn't go off and there was traffic," I said so low, so soft, my voice was almost a whisper.

He took another step closer, and I forced myself not to move one back. I felt his body heat slam into me, felt my pulse race and between my legs become wet. I did take a step back then, and another, and another, until I felt the wall stop my retreat. And the entire time, Jareth followed me.

"You should be reprimanded for being late." He dipped his gaze down to my mouth, and I involuntarily licked my lips. A deep groan left him, my pussy creaming even more in response. I clenched my thighs together, the arousal so pronounced I had a hard time breathing.

"Reprimand me?" There was no point in acting like I had my shit together, like I wasn't completely lost in Jareth. What was the point of pretending when he could read me better than I could probably read myself?

"Disciplinary action should be taken," he said and stepped closer to me so that our bodies were only an inch apart.

"And what would that be?" My voice was no more than a whisper—a very aroused, erotic whisper.

"I don't know, Sofie. Maybe I should just show you instead of tell you."

I moaned softly after he spoke. I was hoping he would say something like that. Maybe he would withhold orgasm, spanking my ass until it was red and sore, or maybe he would make me suck him off, force me to swallow all his cum like a good little girl. God, the thoughts in my head would, *could* be my undoing, could have gotten me off right then and there.

But it was long moments before he said anything else. He didn't even touch me, didn't even make a move like he would. "Pull up your skirt and show me your panties."

My heart was racing so hard and fast it was

actually painful. "I'm not wearing panties." God, was that my voice? It was sexy and sultry all in the same breath.

A deep grunt left him, and he moved another inch closer to me. "What a good girl you are." He looked down at my mouth again. "Do what I say, Sofie."

I reached down and grabbed the edge of my skirt, pulling up the material. It was a pencil design, formfitting, causing me to wiggle my hips in order to get the material up my thighs.

Once the fabric was above my hips, I watched as Jareth looked down to the area between my legs. I had thigh-high stockings on, the straps attached to a garter, the outfit I'd worn because I knew Jareth liked it, and because it made me feel sexy as hell.

"Spread your legs," he said demandingly.

I did as he ordered, spreading my legs, the cool air moving along the most intimate part of me.

"You know I like how smooth your pussy is."

I nodded. Although I waxed my pussy because I liked the way it felt, especially during sex.

"Turn around," he said, and I did exactly that, looking over my shoulder and seeing his focus trained down. "Look at that ass. By the time you leave this office, you'll be weak-kneed and begging me to fuck you, Sofie."

I closed my eyes and rested my head on the wall, moaning softly. Yes. That's exactly what I wanted.

"Turn around," he ordered.

I did as he said.

For long moments, Jareth didn't speak; he just stared at me, looked me in my eyes, the control he had over this situation evident. And although I was a strong woman in my own right, independent and successful, I couldn't help but admit that having Jareth in control like this turned me on.

He lowered his gaze to my bare pussy, his face like stone, his breathing even. He had his desire and control in check; that was evident. But then again, he always did.

"I want you to touch yourself, to move your hand down to your pussy and spread your lips for me."

My belly was hollowing in and out at his command, and I obeyed instantly. Moving my fingers down my belly, over the material of my skirt, and finally over my smooth mound, I stopped right before I fully touched myself.

"Be a good girl for me, baby," he growled low.

Here he was, dressed impeccably, his hands still in the pockets of his slacks, his voice only showing the barest hint of arousal, and his gaze trained right on my pussy.

He acted so... in control. And I felt anything but.

I touched my clit at first, a small gasp leaving me. I moved a digit down my center, feeling how soaked I was, how wet my pussy was for Jareth.

"Show me more," he demanded, but his voice was even.

I leaned my back against the wall, lifted my hips up slightly, and spread my lips wide so he could get a good look at me.

For a moment, he said nothing, didn't move—hell, I didn't even think he breathed.

"You're so wet," he said, and in that moment, he couldn't hide the gruffness that laced his voice.

I shifted so I could dip my gaze to the crotch of his slacks, could see the massive outline of his erection pressing against the expensive, custom-tailored material, and I grew lightheaded.

"Rub your clit. I want you to almost get off, Sofie." He looked into my eyes once more. "But you wait for me to give you permission to go over the edge." There was a harsh growl in his voice. "I want you to take yourself almost there and then stop."

Oh. God.

I started rubbing myself, closed my eyes, and just gave in to the pleasure.

"Look at me," he ordered.

I forced myself to open my eyes and look into Jareth's. He took a step forward, and I felt his body heat move against me. I parted my lips and gasped at the sensation, loving the feeling, wanting more. Needing it.

"Rub yourself faster," he said softly and leaned his face in just an inch. I could feel his warm, peppermint-smelling breath against my lips and I moaned for more. "Harder, Sofie."

A small cry spilled from me as I felt that peak coming closer, almost within reach. The light sheen of sweat started lining my spine, but in the back of my mind, I knew I couldn't come, not without Jareth's permission.

"I'm... so close." I whispered those words harshly, pleading, begging with my eyes for him to give me what I wanted. But he said nothing, just stared at me, just made me continue to rub myself. I tried desperately, in vain, not to get off.

When I knew I couldn't stop myself, couldn't control it, his hand grabbed my wrist, stopping me. My inner muscles clenched, my orgasm right at the surface, threatening to spill over, to disobey Jareth's orders. He was breathing harder, his arousal evident now no matter how much he tried to control it.

We stared into each other's eyes, and I could feel the hard outline of his cock against my thigh. He pressed his dick against me a little firmer, dry humping himself against me... using me like I wanted.

But he was a master at control, at waiting. With his fingers wrapped around my wrist, he pulled my digits away from my clit, lifting my hand up so it was now between us. And still, he stared into my eyes as he opened his mouth and sucked those digits in.

I felt his tongue swirl around the pads, licking all my juices off, all of my arousal. I tried to clench my thighs together, but he had his knee wedged between them, forcing them to stay open, knowing what I wanted, needed, but denying me.

And God, did that turn me on even more.

When he was done sucking my fingers clean, he slipped them from his mouth, placed my hand over his cock, and then leaned in and kissed me. He shoved his tongue in my mouth, making me taste myself on him. I curled my fingers around his dick and rubbed him through his pants, wishing he'd come for me.

He had me on the verge of begging him to fuck me right here, right now.

But he broke the kiss far too soon, took a step back, and left me feeling bereft.

"Next time, you'll be on time, won't you, sweet girl?"

I nodded.

"Next time, I'll let you get that reward for being a good girl, Sofie." I watched as he adjusted his cock and moved back behind his desk, sitting down, being the CEO he was. "If you're a good girl the rest of the day, I'll reward you tonight, baby girl."

I slumped against the wall and moaned out my disappointment.

"Pull your skirt back down, right yourself, and get back to work." Although his tone was demanding, authoritative, there was also gentleness to it.

And as I adjusted my skirt, my pussy and inner thighs soaked from my arousal, the discomfort a reminder of what I'd almost had, what Jareth had refused to give me, I knew once we were alone, in his apartment, he'd give me everything I needed.

Everything I wanted.

CHAPTER FOUR

Sofie

I was sore, exhausted, but the pleasure I felt through every single cell of my body, every synapse, made me feel... alive. But I always felt like this after being with Ryker and Jareth.

They played my body like they were maestros and I was their orchestra.

I never felt more empowered than when I was with them. And it was for different reasons, different feelings.

I moved faster, my sneakers eating up the asphalt as I ran around the lake. This was lap two, but I wouldn't stop until I was drenched in sweat, until my legs ached and my knees felt like pudding. Only then would I stop. Only then would I allow myself to take a break.

This was my day of not seeing them, my choice, my decision. I created the schedule, the routine. But it worked out for all of us, worked out so perfectly that we were all like a fluid machine.

I pumped my arms and legs harder. I passed a woman walking her dog, the Labrador barking at me, pulling on the leash. There was a woman with her child in a stroller, her cell phone pressed to her ear as she argued with someone.

I kept running, kept thinking about my men, how complicated but easy this all was. In a perfect world, I'd have both of them at the same time, not sexually, but where we didn't have to split up the days, where we were all together.

I could picture one on each side of me as I held their hands and we walked around this very pond. Of course, we'd get looks, stares. There'd be whispers, assumptions. But to be honest, I didn't care about any of that. I just wanted Ryker and Jareth in my life always.

It was selfish, I admitted, and a part of me felt guilty for that, for making them have to be okay with sharing because I didn't want to let them go. But was I really making them do anything?

They were grown men, adults, and could make their own decisions about if they wanted to stay in this relationship or not, even if it was complicated at times, unorthodox, to say the least.

I was rounding my second lap when my music was interrupted by an incoming call. I slowed my pace to a jog and checked my phone, seeing it was my mom.

"Hi, Mom," I said once I answered the call.

"Hi, honey. What are you doing?"

I panted. "Running."

"Oh good. I thought I'd called during something else."

I rolled my eyes and chuckled. "Mom, please don't go there."

"What? I mean, how am I supposed to know your schedule since you have Ryker and Jareth every other day?"

Oh my God. I slowed my run and started walking, not sure what to say, regretting even saying anything to my mom right from the beginning.

"Mom, we're not fiends, good lord." I snorted and shook my head.

"Well, excuse me." My mom had a teasing note in her voice. "Besides, you know I'm just giving you a hard time. If I don't do it, who will?"

I laughed softly. "I guess that's true, but still, nobody wants to hear their mom even mention sex." I internally cringed at the very thought of that. Although my mother and I were close, became even closer after my father left, my sexual life was not something we delved into. Or hers.

I walked half the pond as I listened to my mother talk about her new position at work, the garden party she'd gone to over the weekend, and how she learned to properly drink tea out of porcelain cups. Then she went into talking about how good the French macaroons were and how she was going to try to figure out how to make them this weekend.

"I wish you lived closer, honey. We could do all these things together."

"Me too, Mom."

After college, I'd moved closer to the city, but stayed right on the outskirts of it. It was a short drive to work, but still gave me a little more privacy than if I was right up in the thick of skyscrapers and shoulder-to-shoulder crowds.

Although it was only a five-hour drive to my mom, both of us were so busy that it meant there wasn't a whole lot of time to commute back and forth.

But we tried to see each other at least once a

month, sometimes once every two months if life was especially hectic.

But ever since her divorce from my cheating father, she'd made herself busy with garden parties, going on vacations with her friends, and just living her best life. It was like my father had been holding her back from who she really needed to be, and once he was out of the picture, she'd opened her wings and flown.

"So I was thinking of coming up for a visit next month, maybe having dinner with you, Ryker, and Jareth? I can make supper, maybe my pasta specialty? Maybe even bring someone?"

I froze. Bring someone? I wasn't even about to delve into that right now.

I focused on visiting with her. I hadn't seen my mom for almost two months now, and it was definitely time. Although she'd met Jareth before, we'd never actually sat down together... the four of us. In fact, it had never been Jareth, Ryker, and myself all in the same room at the same time. It wasn't that I thought they wouldn't get along, but I guess because it all seemed so... weird and unconventional?

I didn't even know if that was the correct word to use, didn't really know the rules on how this all played out. It wasn't like I'd ever done this before. I'd only ever been with two men my entire life, and those were Ryker and Jareth. I was madly in love with both of them, so that's why I was selfish as hell when it came to picking only one. That's why I wouldn't, *couldn't* do it.

Although I knew the guys were fine with the way things were, having all of us in the room might seem weird. Would things be tense, awkward? Or maybe this was for the best. Maybe having all of us in the room would really shed light on if this triad relationship would actually work.

I guess there was only one way to find out, and that was to go through with this and hope shit didn't hit the fan. Because the very thought of things not working out, of losing the two men who completed me fully, was too painful to even think about.

CHAPTER FIVE

Sofie

Ryker slipped his hand in mine as we walked past shops. I looked up at him, feeling a smile spread across my face. I loved it when my big, strong man did sweet little moments of PDA with me. Although I'd love to be in bed with him, his big body wrapped around mine, doing nothing but sexy stuff for the next three days as we got lost in pleasure, I couldn't deny these mundane things we did were also pretty damn incredible.

He'd picked me up and surprised me with lunch at this brand new little bistro on the outskirts of town, and after that, we'd driven to the new ritzy shopping plaza. He wasn't the type of guy who particularly liked being all social, especially at a mall, but I knew he'd taken me here because he remembered me talking about it a few months back. It was these little things that endeared me to him, that my hardened, biker boyfriend showed me that he had a soft side, that he remembered the little things I said in passing.

And although I knew that, had experienced it countless times, there were moments it was easy to forget, because he was alpha all the way.

"Come on," he said in that deep voice of his that always had shivers racing up my spine. He gave my arm a little tug as he led us in the other direction.

"Where we going?"

He looked down at me and gave me a wink, one that had me thinking completely inappropriate thoughts.

Before I knew it, he was leading us toward this designer boutique dress shop, one that I knew about, one I'd obsessed over. I was also very aware of the price tags on most of their items.

I stepped into the shop and instantly smelled lavender and patchouli. I wrinkled my nose and heard Ryker laugh beside me. When I looked up at him, I saw him grinning.

"Smell get to you?"

I looked around to make sure I didn't say anything loud enough somebody could hear and most likely get offended. "Patchouli," I said in a low, disgusted voice. "Reminds me of man sweat."

Ryker chuckled again and wrapped his arm around my waist, pulling me in close. "I thought you liked the smell of man sweat." There was a teasing, heated tone to his voice.

I felt my cheeks heat at his words. "I only like the smell of man sweat when it's us in bed and you're on top of me."

He growled low, and I felt a shiver race up my spine.

"I'd be careful, Sofie." He leaned in close so his lips were right by the shell of my ear. "I'm half tempted to take you back to the SUV and fuck you in the back like old times."

"Ryker," I whispered, shocked but also aroused. God, I felt my face grow even hotter as I looked around to make sure the sales associates hadn't heard. I glanced at the front desk and saw two young girls standing behind it, both of them gazing longingly at Ryker. I was used to people staring at him though. He was big and tattooed, a little scary-looking even. But I knew that wasn't why they were eye-fucking him. He was so damn attractive and had this bad boy thing going on. You'd have to be blind not to be drawn to that.

I saw the girls start talking softly to each other, but then it seemed like they were almost arguing. Then one of them finally moved away from the sales counter and walked toward us. No doubt they were fighting over who would get to talk to Ryker. He still had his arm around my waist, his fingers curled possessively against my hip. I was small compared to him, only five-foot four compared to his six and a half feet. He towered over me like a beast, with muscles stacked upon muscles.

"Hi," the girl said in a very chipper voice. "Welcome to Chanel DuBois. Is there something I can help you with?"

Although this was a woman's clothing store, she never once took her gaze off Ryker. I would've chuckled if I weren't slightly annoyed. But I couldn't blame the girl. I mean, look at him.

"Well," he said in his deep voice, "I don't think anything would fit me in here, but my girl here definitely wants something."

The sales associate finally turned her gaze to me, raking her eyes up and down my body as if sizing me up, maybe wondering why he was with me. I didn't take offense to it though. It was the look we mainly got when he and I were together.

Jealousy was an ugly thing, especially coming from other women, but I was confident in the love Ryker had for me, knew I satisfied him and he was devoted to me. Other women and their pettiness didn't bother me at all. Not anymore, at least.

"Oh, something for your sister?"

I actually did laugh then. *That's the furthest thing from the truth, sweetheart.* This was the first time someone had thought I was his sister. I didn't know what kind of sibling relationship they thought we had, given the fact that he had his arm wrapped around me, but whatever.

"She's far from my sister."

Looked like Ryker was having the same thought process as me.

He pulled me even closer against his body. I rested my head on his arm and looked at her, smiling sweetly. The young woman cleared her throat and nodded, her cheeks becoming pink.

"A special occasion?"

Ryker shook his head as he stared at her. "Nah. I just want to treat my girl."

I could see from her expression she knew things were going to go nowhere with Ryker, so she slipped on a professional expression and started pointing out the casual clothes, and then the more dressier things.

"We want those," he said, tipping his chin toward the intimate apparel section. Ryker slipped his hand in mine and we headed toward the back.

He let go of my hand and started going through the racks, pulling off two scanty pieces of lace and turning to finally look at me. My face was on fire by this time, and I looked over my shoulder to see the two girls looking at us curiously.

"Try these on for me." His tone was a little demanding, and a lot arousing.

I walked up to him and took the two hangers out of his hand, looking over each piece. "Ryker," I said, looking up at him, my eyebrows raised. "These are nothing more than straps and lace." I glanced back down at them. "This isn't going to cover anything." When I looked back at him, I could see he liked that just fine. His gaze spoke volumes.

"That's the point, Sofie."

"Oh," I said softly. Lord, was I that dense?

I cleared my throat and looked at my shoes, feeling embarrassed even though I knew I shouldn't be. I saw movement to the side and lifted my gaze to see Ryker waving over one of the sales associates.

"We need a dressing room so she can try these on."

The girl glanced between us and the tiny pieces of lingerie I held in my hand. She cleared her throat and nodded, clearly feeling a little bit embarrassed given the subject matter.

"There are some in the back. No key needed to get in them. Let me know if you need any help," the sales associate said and all but scurried off, as if she knew she didn't want to be here for this next bit.

I turned and faced Ryker, lifting an eyebrow and giving him no doubt a curious look. "Seriously?"

He crossed his arms over his broad chest and nodded once.

"Come on, baby. Let me see how you look in them."

God, we were really doing this... and it excited me.

CHAPTER SIX

Sofie

I stared at him for a suspended moment, seeing if maybe he would relent and not make me do this. But the truth was I kind of liked how he was pushing this, wanting to see me in the lingerie.

I made my way into one of the dressing rooms. They were located in the back, giving us some privacy from the sales associates and the front desk.

I pulled the curtain closed once I was inside the small room and looked at myself in the full-length mirror. Then I looked down at the lingerie. I felt this flush move over me. My nipples tingled as I imagined the delicate fabric on my sensitive skin. I felt my pussy get wet at the image of Ryker taking the material off me.

Breathing out slowly, the knowledge that he was waiting right outside, ready to see what it looked like, had arousal moving fast and frantically through my body.

I got undressed and put the first one on, stared at myself in the mirror, and felt extremely sexy, almost erotic. Here we were in a clothing store, just a thin piece of material separating Ryker and myself, people just feet away, and I was scantily dressed.

"Sofie," Ryker said in a voice clearly laced with pleasure. "Show me, baby." He said it a little bit lower so only I could hear, so only I could know where his thoughts were obviously going.

I turned around and reached out to grab the curtain, pulling it aside, the metal rings on the pole sliding softly. I stood there for a moment staring up at him, watching as his eyes raked me up and down from toe to head and back down to my toes.

The black lace lingerie was literally nothing but scraps of material and strings of silk. The silk weaved around my body, braiding along my sides in a feminine manner, accentuating my curves. A minuscule triangle of lace covered my mound, and my ass was all but hanging out. The silk moved up the length of my spine to wrap around my breasts almost innocently.

Hiding but showing.

Tempting but denying.

I was breathing harder and faster, my belly hollowing in and out the longer I stood there, the longer the silence stretched out. I chanced a glance down at his jeans, feeling my eyes widen at the massive erection pressing against the denim. I licked my lips and slowly trailed my gaze back up his abdomen, looking into his face and seeing that he already watched me.

"Ryker." I breathed out his name.

And then he took a step toward me, and another one until he was in the dressing room, crowding me, taking up the entire space. Without breaking eye contact with me, he reached behind him and grabbed the curtain, pulling it slowly closed.

I was frozen as I watched Ryker lift his hand, then felt him trail his finger lightly along one of the silk straps on my shoulder, following it over my bustline, and continuing lower until he was tracing the braided design on my side.

Every part of me tingled, and in that moment, we weren't in the shop; we weren't just feet from other people. We were alone, in this private, secluded setting, just he and I, the perfect setup for the erotic things I wanted him to do to me.

"Show me the next one," he said matter-of-factly and took a small step back. "Undress, Sofie."

I wanted his hands back on me, wanted him to touch every single inch of me.

I kept my gaze locked on his as I undressed, as I set the delicate piece of lingerie on the bench behind me and reached for the red one. I was completely nude at this point, my body on full display for him. As I looked into his eyes, saw the way he glanced down at my breasts then lower to my bare pussy, I felt a gush of moisture leave me, my body preparing for him.

This red piece of lingerie was crotchless, and the filthy part of my brain couldn't help but imagine what we could do easily because of that, how no one would hear us or see us as I wore this scrappy little piece of material and Ryker did whatever he wanted to me.

Once I was dressed, I stood there motionless, hardly even breathing. Ryker had his hands on my hips a moment later, lifting me easily so my feet were flat on the seat. Our faces lined up perfectly, the scent of his cologne, of his need, slamming into me.

He leaned in slowly so his lips were now right by my ear, not touching, but his breath moving along the shell.

"The things I want to do to you right now," he rumbled out softly, and I felt the tip of his nose trail lightly along my jawline. He slid his hand between my thighs, his breathing increasing when he finally touched me down there. A moan almost spilled from me, but I stopped it, biting my lip, telling myself we weren't truly alone.

I could hear a stuttering breath leave him. "So wet. God, you're so wet."

I closed my eyes and rested my head back against the mirror, my knees shaking, the only thing holding me up being Ryker's hand between my thighs and his body pressed against mine.

"Fuck me," I whispered, the words coming from me before I could stop them. "Right here, right now. Fuck me."

He rested his forehead on my shoulder and groaned deeply, slipping a thick finger inside of my pussy. My mouth opened on its own, a breathless sound leaving me.

"As much as I want to, I'm too possessive and selfish to do this where someone could hear us. I need you all to myself, Sofie. I need you alone." He pulled his finger from me, and I made a sound of disappointment.

I opened my eyes to see him lifting his hand, the digit glossy from being shoved deep inside me. He moved it toward my mouth. With my eyes locked on his, I opened, sucking that finger between my lips, sucking my cream off, knowing it turned him on.

He had his hands back on my hips, helped me off the seat, but he didn't let go of me for long seconds. I licked my lips again, not trusting my voice in that moment.

"Which one did you like better?" My voice was shaking as I forced those words out.

He didn't answer for a prolonged minute, just stared into my eyes, making me feel so on edge, so uneasy in the best of ways.

"We're going to get them both." He leaned in. "How can I decide on just one when I've seen what you look like with both of them on?" He took my hand and placed it over his cock. "When you've done this to me in a matter of seconds, Sofie?" He was rock-hard, like granite behind his fly.

He lifted his other hand and cupped my chin with his thumb and forefinger, tilting my head back, staring at my mouth. I thought he'd kiss me, but he was prolonging this, making me wait.

"Get dressed and I'll meet you at the front desk." He leaned back, and I tried to catch my breath. "Because if I stay in here with you, I'm liable to push you against the glass, bend you over, pop out that perfect peach ass of yours, and shoved my dick home, Sofie." He stared in my eyes. "Tonight, baby. Tonight."

My lips parted slightly. Before I could say anything in return, beg him to do just that, Ryker was out of the dressing room, the curtain back in place, and I stood there wondering what in the hell had happened.

The only thing on my mind now was getting back to his place so he could deliver on his promise.

Ryker pulled into his driveway, cut the engine of his Tahoe, and we sat there in silence for a few moments. The backseat was filled with shopping bags, the day spent with Ryker lavishing and spoiling me. But my gaze kept going to the little black bag that was set off to the side, the one that held the lingerie, memories of that dressing room playing on repeat in my head.

I looked over at him, could see his hands were

still wrapped around the steering wheel, his focus trained straight ahead. He seemed tense, but not in a bad way, more so in the trying to control those sexual urges way.

And honestly, I'd been the same way since leaving the dressing room.

That excited me, because I knew why he was like that, knew he'd been thinking about it as much as I had.

But we finished out the day normally, no excessive PDA, no more almost fucking in a dressing room. We'd been good, behaved.

And damn had it been hard.

But toward the end of the day, I felt that control slipping, especially from Ryker. I pictured how he looked as he sat across from me at the table when we'd eaten dinner. He'd watched me like a starving predator. He'd watched me like I was the only thing he wanted to sate that hunger.

His possessiveness had been tangible. Hell, he'd even snapped and glowered at the waiter when he smiled at me.

"Ryker?" I reached out to place my hand on his denim-clad thigh. He looked over at me, shifting on the seat so he was facing me now. "Thank you for today. It was wonderful spending time with you." I moved my hand up and down his thigh, not to be sexual, but that's exactly where my thoughts led.

The way he watched me said his mind was right there with mine.

"You enjoyed yourself?" His voice was so husky, so deep, like he had to force it to work.

I nodded. "So much, and it was made even better because you were there." The pitch of my voice became more sultry, needy.

He stayed silent for several moments, and then he cupped my cheek, smoothing his finger along my skin.

Ryker was so gentle with me, but I knew him well enough to know he was only like this with me. Over the years of all but growing up with him, I remembered plenty of fights he'd gotten into. And they'd all been because he felt a guy was disrespecting me, sexualizing me.

Blood had been shed, bruises formed, bones broken. He was unapologetic about it too. He was protecting me, my honor, and how could a girl be mad at that?

I looked back at his house, thinking about his bedroom, the couch, even the kitchen table. We'd done it on just about every surface imaginable, and every time, it was like the first. Every time, it was exciting and new and had me anxious for more.

When I turned and looked at him, my mouth parted, but before I could tell him that we should head inside, his expression had any words stilling on the tip of my tongue. He slipped his hand around my nape, pulled me forward, and slammed his lips down on mine.

I instantly melted against him, opening my mouth wider and slipping my tongue against his, moaning at the flavor and feel of him. He had his other hand on my hip, intermittently squeezing me as if he were trying to calm himself, trying to ground himself.

And before I knew what was happening, I was pulled on top of him, the steering wheel pressed into my back, and Ryker's hard, muscular chest pressed against mine.

"I've been wanting this all day," I said after we broke the kiss, both of us panting, Ryker's hands on my hips as he squeezed me, pulling me closer. I could feel how hard he was between my thighs, that thick length begging to be released.

He didn't say anything in response, but he didn't have to. I could see in the way he was looking at me and how hard his body was that I was affecting him, that he was right here with me.

I pressed my lower half down against him, grinding myself on his erection, loving that my big, strong biker was trying in vain to act like he had any kind of control.

Because we both knew that once he let go, all bets were off. Once he said fuck trying to go slow, the real Ryker would come out to play.

CHAPTER SEVEN

Ryker

I wanted to make this good for her, to have her spread out on my bed, her hair a dark mass atop my white pillowcases. I wanted her naked and ready for me, her legs spread, her knees bent.

I wanted to fuck her all night.

I was so far gone in this moment. Ever since the dressing room incident earlier today, it was all I'd been thinking about. This moment. When I'd have her all alone, all to myself.

I craved Sofie like no other, needed her like I needed oxygen. She was mine, and I was hers. And that's how it would always be. In the back of my mind, I knew she had Jareth, but none of that mattered. Because when she was with me, when it was just us... she was mine.

If being with Sofie meant I had to share her with another, I was more than okay with that. I was more than willing, because I wanted her happy. Above all else, that's what mattered.

I slipped my hands up her arms, over her shoulders, and cupped both sides of her neck, tilting her head back slightly, watching as her lips parted. Her pupils were dilated, her eyes half-closed as desire moved across her face, a visual showcase of how far gone she really was.

She was primed for me; I had no doubt about that. Hell, I could practically feel how wet she was through our jeans. I wanted her soaking, wanted her drenched on top of me, her arousal slipping down my cock, the wet sounds of us fucking filling the interior of the Tahoe.

Yeah, I wanted all of that and more. So. Much. More.

She leaned in and kissed me softly, almost sweetly. And although I loved that about her—I loved everything about her—right now, I wanted real. Fucking. Dirty.

I had my hands on her hips, squeezing her to me,

pulling her down on my dick as I lifted my hips up slightly. I ground myself against her, used my hands on her to start rocking her back and forth over my cock, both of us dry humping the fuck out of each other as we made out.

Her moan was soft, pleasure-filled, and was like gasoline on my arousal. I growled in response.

I fucked her with my tongue, pushing the muscle in and out of her mouth, making her take it before retreating and sucking hers back into my mouth. My cock was so hard, digging against my zipper, demanding to be free. My balls were drawn up with the need to fill her with all of my cum so it dripped out of her pussy riding me hard.

She broke away and panted, and all I wanted to do was pull her back in, make her kiss me again, give her everything that I was.

"Ryker," she moaned and closed her eyes, using her own momentum to rock herself on me, grinding her pussy against my erection.

"That's it, baby," I groaned harshly.

We were kissing again as I moved my hands between our bodies and started undoing the button of her jeans and pulling the zipper down. She broke away, panting, rising up enough that we could push her jeans and panties over her ass and down her thighs. It was an awkward, almost laughable teenage scenario to try to get them off in the cab of the Tahoe, but once the material was pulled off and hanging from one of her legs, she was straddling me again.

The heat of her pussy speared right into my cock. Fuck, I could feel it, practically feel her wetness soaking through the denim.

"Ryker, fuck me," she moaned against my mouth, and I grunted in response.

I felt feverish, lost in her. I felt rough and raw, and knew this wasn't going to be a sweet and gentle lovemaking session in my bedroom. This was going to be hard and fast and primal. Dirty, sweaty, and explosive. Right now, that's what we both needed.

"What do you need, Sofie? Tell me exactly what you want and it's yours." I wanted her to be filthy, to be crude and vulgar.

I slipped my hands up her sides, cupped her breasts, felt her hard little nipples pressing through the material of her shirt, and trailed my fingers up to cup the sides of her face. I pulled back and looked into her eyes, this hazy, drugged-out expression looking back at me. She was so damn beautiful when she was lost in pleasure.

"Take it out, Ryker. Take out your cock and fuck me right here."

My heart was racing, my throat tight, and my palms sweating. I was trying to act like I was in control, but I finally just said fuck it.

I had my hands between our bodies and was pulling down the zipper of my jeans, not even bothering with the button. I reached down and pulled my cock out, the fucker big and thick, long and rock-hard. Pre-cum lined the tip, my need for her so evident I probably could've gotten off just by staring at her.

She leaned back slightly, as much as she could, given the fact that the steering wheel was behind her, and looked down at my cock in my hand.

"You like seeing what you do to me?"

She nodded.

I started stroking myself from root to tip and back down, staring at her face, watching as her mouth parted, seeing the pleasure on her face as she stared at me jerking off. But I had to stop myself or I'd come, would end this before it really started.

"Do you want this, baby?" She licked her lips, her gaze hazy as she breathed out her affirmation. "Tell me how bad you want it. Tell me how bad you want my dick shoved so deep in your pussy you won't be able to sit comfortably tomorrow."

Her breathing was fucking hard, her chest rising and falling, her breasts pressed against her T-shirt.

"Why don't you touch my pussy and see how wet I am to know how much I want it, how much I want you?"

Christ.

I let go of my cock and slammed my mouth on her, kissing her brutally. She had her hands between my legs and was the one stroking my shaft now, her fingers small and delicate, smooth and so unlike mine.

I grabbed her bare ass, squeezing the supple, perfect flesh. "Place that pussy right over my cock. Slide that cunt on me, baby."

Sofie moved her hands from between our bodies and gripped my forearms, rocking back and forth on my cock. Fuck, she was so damn soaked. I ran my tongue along her lips, the small little gasp she gave me causing my cock to jerk. She tasted fucking good, incredible. Sofie rocked faster and harder, her pleasure evident on her face. All I could do was watch her, mesmerized by the sight of how good she looked as she tried to reach her pleasure, as she tried to get off.

"Use me, baby."

"God, Ryker," she moaned out as she tipped her head back and closed her eyes, her body moving fluidly over me.

"That's it, baby. Ride that sweet little cunt on me. Make yourself come." My voice was strained, thick and heavy with my own desire, my own need to come.

She leaned in and placed her mouth on mine again, gasping and moaning, crying out. I knew she was close. I wanted her to use my body for her pleasure, to get off as she moved against me. My pleasure could wait. This was about her. This would always be about Sofie.

She moved even faster then. I still had my hands on her ass, pulling her forward and pushing her back on my cock, over and over again.

She opened her mouth with a cry, and I knew she was coming for me. I knew she was about to finally give me what I'd craved all fucking day.

Her surrender.

CHAPTER EIGHT

Ryker

To be honest, I didn't have any fucking clue how we even found ourselves in my bedroom. Everything was a damn blur of ecstasy and hazy desire, my cock so hard the fucker felt like it was going to explode unless I came.

Sofie was on the bed, naked, her legs spread, her dark hair fanned out over my pillow. Just like I imagined, just like I craved.

Fuck, she was gorgeous.

And so I stood there for long seconds, my cock in my hand, my focus trained on her pussy. I'd made sure to turn the lights on as soon as we'd gotten to the bedroom, because no way in hell was I going to have shadows concealing her from me.

"Spread wider, baby," I growled, the possessiveness in my voice evident.

She braced her upper body on her elbows, her cheeks flushed, her pupils dilated as she stared at me.

And then she spread for me, parted those creamy, perfect legs of hers, her feet flat on the bed, her pussy on full display.

I was back to stroking my cock, moving the palm of my hand over the head, smearing the pre-cum around, using it for lubrication. I could hear how harsh my breathing was, and I was damn proud of myself for keeping it together as much as I was.

Because what I wanted to do was mount her right here and now, shove my dick inside of her and fill her up with my cum, make her smell like me, and watch as it slipped out of her pussy and made a wet spot on the sheets underneath her.

I lowered my head slightly but kept my gaze trained on her, knowing that I probably looked primal, unhinged. Hell, that's how I felt.

I took a step forward, and then another, and one more until I was right there on the edge of the mattress, the scent of her arousal slamming into me and pulling a groan from the center of my chest.

"Reach down and pull your pussy lips apart. Let me see how pink your center is, Sofie." I didn't even recognize my own voice.

The small sound that escaped her told me she was probably just as surprised by all of this is I was. But she listened so beautifully, sliding her hand down her flat belly, over her hipbones, and finally framing her pussy.

She had her fingers on her lips, pulling the flesh apart, showing me exactly how pink she really was, how wet she was. Sofie was soaked, drenched. And it was all for me.

As much as I wanted to eat her out, lap up her pussy juices, and make her get off against my mouth, I was too far gone for any of that.

I had to have her right now.

I crawled up on the bed, my hands on either side of her waist, my nails digging into the sheets. I looked down between her thighs, could see my cock pointing straight at her, thick and long, ready to fill her up. She went to touch me, but I made a gruff sound and shook my head.

"Baby, if you touch me right now, I'm liable to come before I even get inside of you." I trailed my gaze up her belly and over her ribs, staring at her perfect tits, marveling at the way her nipples were this rosy red color and so damn hard.

I bet they were tight for me, begging for my mouth on them.

Oh fuck it.

I leaned down and sucked a tip into my mouth, moving my tongue around it, feeling it pucker even more. She moaned softly, thrusting her chest out as if she couldn't stop herself, as if she were trying to get more of her breast against me.

I cupped her other breast, moving my thumb along her nipple, pulling at it, tweaking it. I felt the heat of her pussy spear right to my cock, and I forced myself to pull back, her flesh popping free of my mouth. I looked down and saw how glossy her skin was, how red from my sucking. I positioned myself between her legs, grabbed the base of my cock, and stroked myself a few times, the tip pointed right at her pussy hole.

The muscles in my abdomen were clenching and relaxing almost violently from how forcefully I was breathing, how hard I was trying to control myself. It was this never-ending battle inside me, as if there was this tug-of-war with reality and my desire whenever she was around.

Even after all this time, it felt like I was giving her myself all over again, as if we were in the back of my car being awkward virgins as we figured out how to do all... this.

Holding on to the base of my cock, I placed the tip right at her entrance, not pushing in despite the fact that I desperately wanted to. I looked at her face, her eyes wide, her mouth parted, and her cheeks pink. "Look at what I'm about to do."

She braced herself on her elbows and looked down the length of her body, right between her legs, right where I was positioned.

"Watch, baby. I want you to see as I claim you." Although this wasn't our first time together, it sure as fuck felt like it. It felt like it all the time. And having Sofie watch as I slid my dick into her tight pussy was such a fucking turn-on it took every ounce of self-control I had not to bust a load right in her belly.

And then I slowly started pushing in as I stared at her face. She was so tight and hot, so wet that a groan came from me before I could stop it.

"Fuck," I breathed out. "That's so fucking good."

Sofie moaned softly and nodded, lying back down and closing her eyes, lifting her hands and spearing her fingers in her hair, the pleasure on her face evident.

"Ryker." She cried out my name when I thrust fully into her, my shaft seated inside her tight cunt, my balls resting against her ass.

We were both breathing hard, and I was frozen in place, letting her adjust to my size, to my penetration. I looked down between our bodies and pulled out slowly, watching as my dick was revealed inch by big inch, my cock glossy from her arousal, her pussy lips spread wide around my girth.

I swore, the sight enough to have the cum nearly exploding out of me, about to fill her up completely.

"Fuck me," she whispered, her eyes half-closed as she watched me, the blue irises seeming to almost glow.

I curled my hands tightly around her waist now, stabilizing her, holding her still for what I was about to do.

And that was exactly what we both wanted, what she'd asked for—to fuck her.

I started thrusting in and out of her, slow and steady at first, but with each passing second, I increased my speed, pounding into her harder.

Sweat started to immediately bead along the length of my spine and chest, and all I could do was focus on her, concentrate on the fact that my cock was tunneling in and out of her tight pussy, and listen to the sounds of her moaning and begging for more. It was a visual and auditory orgasm in itself, enough to make me nearly get off from that alone. But I wanted her to climax first. I wanted Sofie to cry out as she came. I wanted to hear her and feel her muscles clenching around my dick as she found her pleasure.

"That's it," I grunted and thrust into her especially hard, hearing a high-pitched cry come from her, and knowing she wouldn't last much longer. Neither would I.

I kept staring at my cock as I thrust back into her. She was scorching hot, soaking wet, and all mine. Over and over, I pumped into her body, practically tasting her on my tongue, feeling that ecstasy start to settle at the base of my spine, the impending feeling of my orgasm approaching. I pulled out of her quickly, hearing her soft groan of disappointment, but not giving her a chance to ask why I'd stopped.

I flipped her onto her belly in a matter of seconds, lifting her lower half up so she was forced to brace herself on her knees. With my hand on the center of her back, I kept her upper body pressed to the mattress. She was face down, ass up, and I was shoving back into her cunt with such force both of us gasped at the same time.

Sofie had her head turned to the side, and I saw how her eyes were closed, her mouth parted as she panted in and out. She clutched the sheets, pulling at them as if she couldn't control herself, as if she were trying to rip them from the very mattress.

I slid my hands down her sides and curled them around the mounds of her ass, digging my fingers against the soft flesh, and then slightly pulling the cheeks apart. She was spread obscenely wide for me, her tiny little asshole on display, the pink perfection of her pussy stretched wide as I pumped in and out of her. I could've come from the sight alone—hell, I could have gotten off from the look on her face as she found her release.

She had that kind of control over me.

But I was holding myself back, waiting until she got off once more. And damn was it hard. It was almost painful not to just let go, to surrender.

"I need you to come again for me, Sofie." I managed to grit those words out, my voice hoarse, almost inhuman from the intensity.

She opened her eyes and looked over her shoulder at me, this hazy, almost drugged-like expression on her face as she blinked, not saying anything but moaning continuously.

"I'm there, Ryker," she whispered, and then she

closed her eyes and opened her mouth to cry out silently.

I felt her clamping down on my cock once more and knew I wasn't going to be able to hold off again.

I started fucking her hard and frantically then, rearing my hips back and slamming forward, my cock tunneling in and out of her perfection.

And that's what she was. Absolute. Fucking. Perfection.

"I love you," I whispered, fucking her, making love to my woman in the way we both desperately needed. I was addicted to her, devoted to her.

She was it for me. The one.

"I love you, Ryker," she responded and closed her eyes again, moaning softly as I continued to claim her.

I looked at her asshole, moved my hand closer, and started rubbing the little hole with my thumb.

"Yes," she said softly, and I snapped my gaze to her face. "More," she begged.

I took her like a madman, dipping my thumb into the tightness of her ass, feeling the ring of muscle open for me as the digit slid inside. And all the while, I kept pushing my shaft in and out of her. That tingling at the base of my spine encompassed my whole body now, and there was no way I could stop my orgasm from rushing to the surface.

"I can't hold back, baby."

"Then don't," she cried out.

I pumped into her once, twice, and on the third thrust, I buried myself to the hilt, exploding inside of her body, filling her up with my seed. I made her take everything, every single last fucking drop. Sweat coated her body, a slight sheen of deliciousness I wanted to lick off. My tongue swelled at the very thought, and I could practically taste her salty sweetness on the tip of it.

"Christ." The lone word came from me before I could even try and stop it.

I tipped my head back and closed my eyes, feeling my muscles grow tight as my orgasm continued to rush through me. It was never ending, this painful yet consuming pleasure that stole everything from me.

And only when it started to fade, when the ecstasy lingered but made me sane once more, only then did I finally pull out of her, my semi-hard, damp cock slapping against my thigh, wet and hot from being deep inside Sofie.

I kept her spread like that for a moment, my hands still on her ass, my focus trained on her pussy.

I pulled my thumb from the tight ring of muscle in her bottom and parted my lips as I watched the thick ropes of my cum start to slowly slip out of her pussy, sliding down her slit and clit.

God, if that wasn't the hottest fucking thing I'd ever seen.

Giving her ass one firm smack, I watched the flesh shake from the force, saw the pink outline of my palm come into view. She collapsed on the mattress fully then, her body looking glossy from the perspiration that covered it, her breathing labored.

I lay beside her, my cock spent as it rested on my thigh. Sleep sounded pretty fucking incredible right then, but I needed to hold her, needed to comfort her after what we'd just done.

I needed that for myself too.

And so I pulled her into my arms, shifting her until her chest was pressed to my side, her arm draped over my abdomen.

"I love you," she whispered, the sleepy tone of her voice telling me that my girl would soon crash. That had me smiling, knowing I was the cause of her exhaustion.

"I love you too, Sofie," I said and kissed the top of her head. "Get some sleep. I'm not going anywhere."

I never was.

CHAPTER NINE

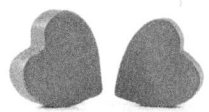

Ryker

I lay on my back with one arm behind my head and my other wrapped around Sofie. I could hear her softly breathing, probably on the verge of sleeping, but she was fighting it, staying in this moment.

Just like me.

"You need to rest, baby." My voice came out in a deep grumble, and she shifted against me. I looked down at her profile. Her nose was small, delicate, her lips full and red. Her cheeks were perfectly arched.

She tipped her head back and looked up at me, her eyes big, blue, gorgeous. I lifted my hand and cupped her face, just staring into her eyes, stroking my thumb along her cheekbone.

"You're perfect," I whispered and leaned down to kiss her on the lips softly, gently. There was no need for anything sexual right now. All I wanted was to be with her, to live in this moment.

"You give me too much credit," she said in response and rested her head on my chest once more.

We stayed silent for long minutes, and I stared at the clock across from the bed, watching the second hand move fluidly to each number.

"What are you thinking about?"

I let her question play between us for a few seconds, let it sink into my mind. I was always honest with her, and right now wouldn't be any different.

I cleared my throat and started to move my fingers up and down her arm, feeling goose bumps break out across her skin. "I'm thinking about you and Jareth together." I felt her tense beside me.

She looked up, her brows knitted in confusion. "You're thinking about us together?"

I chuckled and shook my head. "Not like that. You always have your mind in the gutter." Although her expression relaxed, I could still see she was curious about what I'd said. "I just meant, I wonder how it is between you two. Is it like how it is with you and me?"

She was silent, and I could see from her expression that she was trying to think of how to phrase it, how to even go about this conversation. "It's not like how it is between you and me," she finally said. She was looking at me, and I could see this was weird for her.

"We don't have to talk about it—"

"No, it's not that," she finally said, and I reached out and took her hand in mine. "I just don't know if this whole thing is weird for you."

"It's not," I said right away, meaning it. "I want to know, because it has to do with you, and anything that has to do with you is my priority." She smiled so fucking sweetly at me, and I didn't stop myself from leaning in and kissing her. I had my hand cupped on her cheek, keeping her close as I devoured her mouth for a few seconds.

When I pulled back, she still had her eyes closed and a small smile on her lips. I just took a moment to watch her, to be mesmerized by the sight of her. She was perfect and gorgeous, everything I ever wanted in a woman. And she was mine.

She opened her eyes and her smile grew. She

had a drowsy expression on her face that made my heart skip a beat. I'd never been much of a sappy guy, but fuck, when it came to Sofie, there was just no getting around that.

"It's not the same, because both of you are so different."

I looked down at her lips. "He gives you what I can't and vice versa." I didn't phrase it like a question, and she nodded. "I get it," I said honestly.

"Can I ask how you're okay with it all?" She sounded genuinely curious.

I stared at the ceiling for a second, letting her question play in my head. When I looked at her again, I could see her focus was trained right on me, could see she held her breath, waiting for my reply.

"Sure, at first I was jealous, but it never really bothered me, if that makes any sense." I looked back at the wall in front of me, thinking about when we talked about becoming official, starting a relationship. Sofie had been open and honest with me from the very beginning, telling me how she wasn't with Jareth, but she felt something between them. This connection, the same thing she felt with me.

And I respected the hell out of that, that she had been truthful right from the start.

Of course, I became envious that she would spend time with someone else if we got together, but then I realized none of that mattered. She loved me, and if that meant I had to share her with someone, strangely enough, I was more than okay with it.

I'd heard people comment on how I was "stronger than most" for letting my woman be with another man while we were together. They'd even called us "freaky" over it all. But none of that fucking mattered, because I didn't think it was weird or crazy, or that it even made me a strong man.

It made me human to want to make the girl I loved happy. Because if she was happy, then so was I.

And it got easier over time, sharing Sofie, my jealousy diminishing, before finally vanishing altogether. I didn't consider being jealous a weakness. It was natural.

Human.

I didn't really think about her with Jareth. I focused on my time with her, when we were together. I was consumed when she was near... obsessed when she was gone.

I never felt like I wasn't enough for her, despite the fact that Jareth could give her what I couldn't.

It just... was.

"It makes me feel selfish, if I'm being honest," she finally said, and I glanced back at her.

"You're not selfish." I said that with such determination I knew she could feel it. There was no way she couldn't. "We all need something, Sofie."

"Yeah, but if you said you wanted to see another woman...." She trailed off, not finishing what she was about to say.

"That won't ever happen. I'm devoted to only you. Just because you need more doesn't mean we all do. I'm content. I feel complete with you. Only you." I wrapped my arm around her shoulders and pulled her in, just holding her, because I could see she was letting this get to her. "How about all of us get together? The three of us?"

She laughed softly. "Funny you mentioned that, because my mom wanted us all to get together so she could bring her new boyfriend over."

"New boyfriend?" I looked over at Sofie and saw her smiling.

"Yeah, she's finally going after what she wants, and I can't wait to meet the guy who caught her attention."

I couldn't help but grin. "Get it, Theresa," I said, and Sofie laughed, which in turn had me chuckling. "I bet he's younger."

Sofie looked over at me. "You think?"

I nodded.

She shook her head. "No way. She'd want an older guy, more secure with his life after the shit she went through with my dad."

"Maybe, or maybe she wants a young buck who can keep up with her newfound insatiable appetite."

"Oh my God, Ryker." She was in a fit of laughter, and I loved hearing it. "You may regret agreeing to get together if that's how it goes down. I'm not about my mom and her PDA."

I tightened my hold on her arm and leaned down to kiss her on the top of her head. "Either way, I'm glad she found someone. She deserves it."

"Yeah, she does."

We lay there in silence, and I sensed Sofie start to drift off to sleep. But I was wide awake, which was perfect, because nothing sounded better than holding her the entire night and not missing a minute with her in my arms.

CHAPTER TEN

Sofie

I shut the front door with my foot, juggling three bags in my arms, and walked into the kitchen to set them on the counter. I'd stopped at the grocery store after work. The closer it got to the dinner—which although was still a few weeks away, seemed like it was right around the corner—I realized I was becoming increasingly nervous the more I thought about it.

Thankfully, my roommate told me she'd be gone for that evening, so I'd have the house to myself when everyone came over, and hopefully shit didn't hit the fan. Obviously my mom had met Ryker before, since we'd grown up together, but it was her first time meeting Jareth. And it would be nice having everyone in the same house, under the same roof—although I still had to ask Jareth.

I started putting things in the fridge but froze when I heard banging coming from down the hall. I straightened, my arm braced on the door of the fridge as I lifted my head and stared at where the bedrooms were.

And there was silence once more, so I started putting the rest of the food away, about to shut the fridge door, when I heard a very distinct, very loud moan.

"Oh my God," I said under my breath and quickly put the last box in the cupboard before folding up the paper bags and putting them off to the side.

I walked out of the kitchen and peeked down the hallway to my roommate's closed bedroom door, hearing another set of moans come through. The banging, coming from what I now knew was the headboard hitting the wall, was loud and powerful, and I felt my eyebrows lift in surprise.

"Damn."

But then everything went silent, a little too quiet, and I straightened, wondering if that was it, if they were done. I was just about to head back into the kitchen and grab the wine coolers I'd bought, when her bedroom door opened and out walked a very naked man.

"Um," I said softly and looked away before I could see anything of importance. Embarrassment and definite discomfort filled me.

"Oh hey," Mr. Naked said. "You must be the roommate." His voice sounded like the stereotypical surfer boy type. "Sofie?"

I nodded but still wasn't looking at him. If this wasn't the most awkward thing to ever happen.

"Lane, get your sweet ass back in here and finish what you started," my roommate called out. "And sorry about this, Sofie. We thought we'd be done and gone before you got home."

I lifted my hand and waved it away, as if she could see me. "Yeah, I'm just gonna grab my drinks and head out to the deck to give you guys... privacy." I went back into the kitchen, grabbed the six-pack out of the fridge, and headed out back to the deck.

Once the back door was shut, I exhaled slowly and shook my head. You'd think having a roommate would mean more run-ins with half-naked men, but this was the first time I'd "caught" her in the act. And she'd never seen me with Jareth or Ryker, since I stayed with them it was at their places.

But now I really felt like I was intruding on her space. Getting my own place was sounding better and better, but with time still on our lease, and me not wanting to fuck her over by leaving, I'd stick it out for the remaining months. I'd given her enough notice that I'd be finding my own place once the lease was up, but looking for an apartment felt stressful and tedious.

Maybe I could convince Jareth and Ryker that we should all move in together?

I snorted at that thought.

I put the six-pack on the small wicker table and sat down, leaning all the way back and staring at the fence that surrounded our tiny as hell, postage stamp back yard. Although I didn't technically live in the city, I was only about ten minutes outside of where the skyscrapers were. The tiny house we rented was in this small allotment, the place really only big enough for one person, given the square footage, but we made it work.

Besides, even with my salary, actually living in the city was a little out of my price range, at least for everything I'd seen for sale or rent.

I rested my head back on the chair and closed my eyes for a minute. Even though it was still a few weeks away, I tried to picture how the dinner would go. We were all adults, so there was no reason to think this would be weird or become awkward. Right?

I think I was more nervous about meeting my mom's new boyfriend, wondering if he was older or younger, if he made her happy. That was my main concern, because she deserved that, deserved to have a nice man who took care of her for once.

I reached over and grabbed a wine cooler, twisting off the cap and setting it aside. And then I tipped the bottle back and took a hearty drink of the strawberry-and-lime-flavored alcoholic beverage. Honestly, I probably could've used something a hell of a lot stronger.

I sat there for long moments, just staring at one of the neighbors in her back yard. She was sunbathing, wearing a skimpy little red bikini as she laid out her towel on her deck, slipped on her Jackie O. sunglasses, and proceeded to put her hair up in a messy bun.

I noticed how she kept looking over her shoulder, and I followed her line of vision to the house next door, where a big, burly man stood by a grill, smoke coming up from whatever he was cooking. He wore a white wifebeater, his biceps huge, his tattoos sporadically placed. He had his longer hair tied up in a bun, similar to the girl right next door. I also didn't miss how he kept glancing over at her, trying not to be obvious, but he really was.

It was funny watching the girl primp before lying down, stretching out her arms above her head, her act of trying to be sexy for the neighbor guy pretty clear.

I could imagine what their lives together would be like, how they'd meet, what they'd say if they talked to each other. I assumed none of that had actually happened, given the fact that they seemed like they were too afraid to even say anything to the other.

She was getting his attention in a flashy, sexy way, and I had to give her props for that. She was taking charge of her life.

And then there was Mr. White Tank Top, trying to act like he didn't notice her. But if I could tell he kept checking her out, no doubt she could as well. Women were intuitive that way.

I brought the wine cooler up and took another long drink. I was about to set it down on the little table beside me when I felt my cell vibrate. Pulling it out of my pocket, I saw my mom's face flash across the screen.

"Hi, Mom," I said and watched as little Miss Red Bikini started putting tanning lotion on her arms and legs. At this point, White Tank Top was turned full around and facing her, a spatula in his hand and his mouth hanging open. I wanted to tell him to watch his meat, because the dark smoke coming up from the grill was starting to be reminiscent of an extinguished campfire.

"Hey, sweetheart. Just double checking that we're still on for dinner."

"Of course, but it's still a ways away, unless you want to make it sooner?"

"No, no, same time is fine. I just want to make sure your schedule hasn't changed. I'm excited for you to meet Trevor."

Trevor. It was the first time she'd said his name. The name Trevor sounded young.

"Yup, still good to go." There was a pause, and then I heard my mother start to giggle. Followed by the rustling of sheets and a distant, low, deep voice.

I sat up straight and felt awkwardness claim me.

Oh my God. Was my mother in bed with her boyfriend right now? Why did she think calling me was a good idea? Why was this my luck? Two uncomfortable sex situations in the span of an hour.

But I was not about to touch on that subject or bring it to light.

Knowing my mom was having sex was at the top of my list of hell nos. Probably the same way she didn't want to know or think about me getting it on.

She started talking about what to bring, even though the dinner wasn't for a while.

"Mom, we have a ways to go still." I laughed softly.

"We need to be prepared, honey."

She went right back to talking about whether to bring a dessert or side dish then started going on about all the things that might be good. And here I was worrying about how everyone would interact, and what her new beau would be like, and she was wondering whether to make a raspberry parfait or bring a cherry cheesecake.

Maybe I was overthinking this. Maybe I was worried for nothing. Maybe I just needed to pull the stick out of my ass and go with the flow, like my mom was apparently doing.

Because what was the worst that could happen?

CHAPTER ELEVEN

Sofie
A couple weeks later

I popped the cap off my lipstick and stared at my reflection in the mirror, smoothing it over my bottom lip first, and then the top. I had my hair in a low bun, little wispy strands framing either side of my face.

I could hear the low thump of music from the event hall, the entire company packed inside the massive room to dance, drink, and eat. It was a celebration of landing one of the biggest deals for the company, and Jareth and the other higher-ups had put together the party as a thank you to everyone. And everyone had helped, in some way, shape, or form.

It didn't matter how small your position was—if you were part of the maintenance department or an executive assistant. We were all equal when it came to working as a team.

We all made an impact on the company, and Jareth and the other bosses wanted to show their thanks and gratitude, which meant one big-ass bash.

I shoved my lipstick in my small clutch, moved a piece of hair away from my forehead, and gave myself a tentative smile. Time really went fast when you're happy, and that's how it was for me, with Ryker and Jareth.

My three days with each of them went by so quickly it was almost as if it didn't even happen. Here I was with Jareth again, my time with Ryker having been incredible but seemingly ended so soon.

That's how it felt each and every time I was with them, and I couldn't help but start to think how it would be if we didn't have to split up.

Our time... if we were all together and there were no rules.

I made my way down the hall, my heels clicking on the polished marble floor. The banquet hall the company had rented out for the evening was ornate and luxurious, with crystal chandeliers hanging from the ceiling, Faberge eggs on display, and a price tag big enough to give somebody a heart attack.

But that was the thing with Jareth and the other bosses. They treated their employees well and showered us with lavish as hell things when the time called for it.

I smoothed my hands down my dress and stepped into the room, the space massive, with a ceiling that resembled a starry night, the fiber optic lights twinkling above. It was gorgeous, more like a piece of artwork than a place to throw a party. But in the city, there were lots of hidden gems.

Although the hidden gems my wallet and I were more familiar with were the off the beaten path pizza joints that were open all night and served beer with the slices.

I glanced around the massive room, everyone mingling, drinks in their hands, waiters in black-and-white attire moving fluidly between everyone with platters of champagne and hors d'oeuvres in their hands. There was a DJ off to the side, up-lighting on every wall, and the whole place almost gave off the feeling that you were at a ritzy wedding reception. A very expensive, very elaborate wedding reception.

I spotted Jareth and a few of the other executives off to the side. No doubt they were talking business. They did that a lot, even if they weren't at work. But I supposed, when you were in a position such as they were, work was everything. It had to be, if they wanted to be and stay as successful as they were.

I stood there just people watching, wondering about their lives, what they were thinking about, what he'd be doing after this. Would some of them go home with each other? Would they let the copious amounts of alcohol they'd been consuming tonight affect their inhibitions?

I looked over at Jareth again, my heart jumping in my throat when I saw he was watching me. He had this intense expression on his face, his focus screaming one thing.

Mine.

Although there were official rules about not having relationships within the company, I knew it was probably frowned upon, because I could imagine the complications a breakup would cause. But nobody talked about it, despite the fact that I knew there were several employees who were getting it on, even sneaking off together during their lunch breaks for a nooner.

And although Jareth and I had never made our relationship official, there was no doubt in my mind that people knew. They had to. It wasn't like things stayed secret for very long. They were just smart enough not to talk about it, because Jareth was the boss.

Jareth said something to his associates and then made his way toward me. I straightened from the wall I was leaning against, my pulse instantly increasing the closer he came.

God, he looked good, with a three-piece suit on, his salt-and-pepper-colored short hair styled away from his face, and an arrogant, sophisticated expression.

He looked good, really damn good, and I was one lucky woman to be able to say he was mine. He stopped only a foot from me, a low growl leaving him as he raked his gaze up and down my body.

"Damn, Sofie, you're looking good enough to eat."

I knew what kind of "eating" he was referring to, and Lord, that sounded incredible.

I felt a shiver rake up and down my spine, felt my nipples start to harden when he kept his gaze trained on my breasts. The dress I was wearing was black and slinky, a silky material that was light and flowed over my body, but it was still form-fitting so you could see my curves. And although I didn't have many of them, I did like to show them off, but only for Jareth and Ryker.

He placed a hand on the wall beside my head and leaned down a little, and even though this probably looked intimate as hell, everyone was too busy right now with their own conversations, getting liquored up, and probably thinking about tonight, to pay any attention to us.

But to be honest, I didn't care what they thought.

I leaned back against the wall and tipped my head up so I could look into his face. "I thought about you when I picked it out to wear tonight," I admitted.

He made another low, gruff sound, and then he was dipping his gaze lower, down my belly, and stopping at the most intimate part of me. "Panties?"

I shook my head slowly. "I'm not wearing any."

He snapped his gaze up to me, and I could practically feel the possessiveness leaving him. "What a good girl, Sofie."

I softened at his praise. "I know what you like, Jareth. I had you in mind when I slipped the dress on, not bothering with panties or a bra, because I wanted you to approve."

When I was with Jareth, that's what I wanted—his approval, because that equated to his arousal, which then led to mine. It was a give-and-take relationship, a power exchange. He controlled me, and that's what I needed. It wasn't an act. It just... was.

Nothing else mattered in that moment, not all these people around us, not the fact that we weren't actually alone. Because it felt like we were. It was just him and me.

He leaned in close and inhaled deeply. I forced myself not to close my eyes and moan, the small act turning me on.

"Do you want a drink?"

I licked my lips and nodded. His voice was smooth, deep, and thick. It reminded me of the whiskey I wanted, the whiskey he'd no doubt get for me, because he knew me well enough.

He gave me a half smile and pushed away from the wall, giving my body one more look up and down before finally turning and heading toward the bar. His movements were fluid, precise. He was like a predator making his way through the crowd. People actually parted for him, moving out of the way. I sighed, a feeling that I was falling down this rabbit hole taking over.

But in this moment, I wanted to fall into the nothingness with Jareth.

He disappeared behind the thick sea of bodies, and I glanced around the room. Several minutes passed before I felt someone approaching, looking at me. Glancing to my right, I saw a man walking toward me, not someone I'd seen at the office before, but then again, he could have been new, an intern, or a plus-one.

He wore a simple black suit with a white button-up shirt underneath, the collar undone. He held a glass in his hand and had a smirk on his face. His focus was trained right on me, and I straightened, looking behind me to see if maybe there was someone else he was directing that grin to. But there was no one behind me except the associates Jareth worked with.

"Hey there," he said a little loudly, clearly trying to make sure I could hear him over the music playing.

I gave him a friendly smile.

"I'm Shawn." He held out his hand and I took it, thinking he'd want to shake it or something, but instead, he brought it to his mouth and kissed my knuckles. I pulled my hand away quickly and a little forcefully and saw the surprise on his face. He held up a hand in mock surrender. "I'm sorry. No harm, no foul."

He cleared his throat and looked away, and a smarter man would have taken the hint and left, but I could practically feel the drunken arrogance pouring from him. He looked back at me with a big, confident smile on his face. I was about to tell him he'd get nowhere with me, but before I could say anything, he started talking again.

"Do you work for the company, or are you a guest of one of the employees?" He leaned against the wall, a little too close for comfort, so I took a step back.

"I work for the company," I said and left it at that. I looked back at the bar for Jareth, but I couldn't see anything but the wall of people clamoring to get another drink.

"What do you do at the company?"

I looked back at him. I knew where this was going and needed to shut it down, because letting him think I was interested in any way was just bad news.

"Listen, Shawn—"

"Before you turn me down, hear what I have to

offer." He grinned wider. He brought his glass up to his mouth and took another drink of the clear liquid, the ice clanking against the side.

"I think you're getting the wrong vibes here." Although I wasn't sure how he could think that, seeing as I sure as hell hadn't led him on. But I knew this type of guy. They were the ones I'd seen in college who were far too cocky for their own good, and getting turned down wasn't something they accepted easily.

He smelled like he'd already had about six of whatever he was drinking, the alcohol coming from his pores strong enough to make me drunk from the fumes alone. That was one of the problems with these gatherings. People tended to really let loose, leave their inhibitions at the door.

"So let me tell you about myself," he said and went right into his spiel before I could stop him. Just walking away sounded pretty good right now, or I could try and hunt Jareth down, but with so many people, we'd end up going around in circles trying to find each other.

"I subcontract for the company and kind of tagged along tonight. So I work for the company, but I'm also a plus-one." He grinned, flashing straight white teeth.

Yeah, he was definitely one of those arrogant guys in school. No doubt he probably flashed those fake pearly whites that had all the girls' panties dropping.

I didn't know if he thought it was going to go on with me, but he was wasting his time.

"I'm taken," I said, but he just kept right on talking. Going on about mergers and acquisitions, numbers and contracts. His salary. Yeah, he actually went there.

I kept searching for Jareth, my mind on the man I loved, and everything else faded away. I was about to tell Mr. I Get Whatever I Want that I wasn't interested and he needed to move along, but I watched as he straightened from the wall and looked behind me.

His expression was guarded... hesitant.

I glanced over my shoulder and felt a shiver race along my skin as I saw Jareth standing right behind me, his big body towering over mine, two drinks in his hands, his focus trained right on Shawn. Jareth looked pissed, and if I was being completely honest, the possessive expression on his face was a little scary.

He handed me one of the drinks, and I didn't miss how he made sure to let his finger slide against my hand, a small, proprietary act that maybe only I noticed, but it was there regardless.

He stepped to my side and wrapped his arm possessively around my waist, but I noticed how his stare was still zeroed on Shawn. Nothing was said, and this thick, weird atmosphere settled around us.

Shawn finally smiled, acting like this was no big thing—although I could see in his eyes as he stared at us that he felt a little uneasy, that he could feel the testosterone and challenge coming from Jareth.

I felt Jareth press his fingers around my hips a little harder, and he pulled me even closer to his body. A low growl left him, and by the look on Shawn's face, I knew he'd heard as well.

The way Jareth was acting right now might have pissed some very independent woman off, but the truth was... I liked it. I grew aroused. I loved it when he got all territorial over me.

"Is there something you needed?" Jareth didn't even know who this man was, but it didn't matter. Shawn could've been the most powerful person in this room, and Jareth wouldn't have given two shits about it. He was staking his claim, letting Shawn know I wasn't up for grabs, that a claim had already been made.

"I was just talking to...." He looked over at me,

just now realizing I hadn't actually told him my name. Shawn cleared his throat and looked back at Jareth. There was some silent communication going on between them, and then Shawn gave a nod, smiled over at me a little uncomfortably, turned, and left.

There was a heavy pause, and I looked over and up at Jareth. His focus was on the retreating Shawn, and another low sound left him, the vibrations going right into my body.

"What was that?" Though, to be honest, I liked this whole barbaric "mine" thing he had going on.

He looked at me as if he couldn't understand what I was talking about, as if this was an everyday occurrence. But then, I supposed it was.

"You know what? Never mind," I said and smiled, rising up on my toes and kissing him in front of everyone. This was the first time I'd been so blatant with PDA concerning Jareth, especially around people we worked with. But in that moment, I didn't care anymore. Why should I? I loved him, and he loved me. It wasn't like people didn't know we were together. I was sure everyone did.

I didn't know if I expected him to push me away, to tell me now wasn't the time, but after his little possessive caveman act just moments before, I was extremely pleased when he wrapped his arm around my waist and pulled me closer to his body. A deep, low sound of need left his chest, the vibrations moving along my skin.

And when he pulled away, I was still on my toes, my eyes shut, pleasure bursting through my veins. All the things I wanted him to do to me slammed through my head. It was only then that I realized there were people watching us, staring openly.

Jareth's co-executives. Employees.

Nearly everyone had their eyes trained right on us. Some had wide eyes of surprise, others had smirks on their faces, and then there were a few who were leaning closer to each other, whispering, probably telling each other "I told you so."

"Let's go back to our place, Sofie."

This would definitely change things in the office, no doubt. Because even if they hadn't known we were together, even if we'd kept our relationship on the down low, this moment right here, right now, had just opened a whole other door.

I felt him cup my cheeks and stroke my skin with his thumb. I opened my eyes and looked into his face, seeing how he was solely focused on me. He'd said "our place," and that's how I felt when I was there, that although I didn't live there fully, he always made me feel like it belonged to both of us.

Ryker and his home were the same way. God, I was a lucky woman.

I didn't verbally say anything, just nodded, feeling my body tingle with awareness, knowing what was to come. And the look on Jareth's face told me this was certainly going to be a night he wouldn't let me forget as he claimed and showed me who I belonged to.

We stepped through his apartment door, and I closed it softly behind me. Ever since he confronted the man who'd been hitting on me, nearly starting a scene, Jareth had been in a strange mood. He'd barely taken his eyes off me, and although I didn't deny I really liked that, I also knew he was feeling pretty territorial.

He went over to the bar and poured us both a drink then turned and walked back to hand me the square glass. The amber liquid inside smelled strong, expensive. Then again, Jareth only got the very best, the rarest and most expensive of liquors. It wasn't to get drunk, but to savor and enjoy.

"You're upset," I said matter-of-factly.

He said nothing as he brought his cup to his mouth and took a small sip. He watched me the whole time, not moving, his big body seeming strung tight, as if he might snap at any moment. Although that "snap" would be in the form of his dominance coming out full-on.

And that thought instantly had me wet.

"I'm not mad," he finally said. A moment of silence stretched between us. "I'm territorial."

I felt my nipples harden painfully, felt myself become even wetter. God, his voice, his words... they were like gasoline on an open fire.

He took a step closer, and I felt myself rooted to the spot, his presence so powerful.

"Tonight... tonight, I need to make it known that you belong to me, Sofie." His voice was a rough grumble. "I'm okay with you and Ryker, but anyone else?" He shook his head slowly. "No. No one else will have you. I'd get savage if it came down to that, Sofie."

I swallowed, my throat so tight, emotions swirling around me so powerful. Someone would say it was weird that Ryker and Jareth were okay with me being with both of them, but when it came to other men, they were too territorial to let me go… to share me.

But I would say love made people do funny but incredible things.

I found myself nodding, because I wanted him to know I agreed, consented.

He took another step toward me, and I thought he would touch me, pull me into the hardness of his body, but instead he stopped, staring at me, almost as if he were thinking about what he'd do to me, picturing it.

And I couldn't help but anticipate every sweet moment of it all.

CHAPTER TWELVE

Jareth

I stared at her for a few seconds and then moved over to my leather recliner pressed against the far wall. I sat my ass down, watching her, the lights dim, causing small shadows to play along her body.

I knew by her expression she was unsure exactly how this would play out, how I'd make her come tonight.

I tried to keep my body calm, my thoughts clear. But whenever I was around Sofie, that was almost fucking impossible. She had this fire burning inside me, one that if not controlled would burn me alive. She'd been the only woman to ever make me feel like this, the only woman to ever make me want something... more.

I'd sworn off women for years before she even came into my life, focused on work.

I kept to myself, built my business, made it the successful empire it was. It was easy to not have the focus of women in my life, because the truth was they'd never done anything for me. Not until Sofie started working for my company and everything else faded away. I would give everything for her. I would sacrifice anything to make sure she was happy.

And that's how I was in this relationship with her, sharing her company with another man, because I knew there were things she needed that I couldn't give her, things her other partner could. That was life; that was human.

And to be honest, it had been hard at first, real fucking hard to share my woman with another man. Jealousy wasn't something I'd ever known before, because what I wanted I took, and if I couldn't take it, I worked my ass off for it.

But this was different. This was my life, my love.

And so when she'd told me about Ryker, asked me how I'd feel if she saw both of us at the same time, there had been no hesitation in me, no desire to end the relationship and stop this. There had been nothing like that, because I loved her and wanted her to be happy.

I moved my thoughts back, tucked them far away. Tonight was about this moment, my woman, and making her feel good. Tonight was about giving her what only I could. That dominance. Her submission.

"Take off your clothes, Sofie." She started breathing harder, her body preparing itself for me. "And get on your knees," I said in a calm, deep voice that brooked no argument.

For a second, all she did was stand there. I saw her pulse beating rapidly right below her ear.

"Do it, Sofie. Do what I say."

I saw the way her hands shook as she started to get undressed, her eyes trained on me the entire time. She knew the rules, knew she was to do what I said, her gaze never leaving mine.

When she had everything off, she just stood there for a moment, the uncertainty of the situation and her lust clear on her face, driving my own arousal even higher.

"On your knees, baby girl, and show me that pretty ass." I said it harder this time, letting her know with my voice that she was starting to disobey.

And then she turned around and sank to her knees.

"Good girl," I praised and lifted my hand, rubbing my palm over my mouth as I stared at her. She had womanly curves, ones I could hold on to as I fucked her. Her body made my mouth water for a taste.

"Show me what's mine." My voice was nothing more than a rough growl at this point. I was leaning back on the chair, the suit I wore feeling constricting, my cock so fucking hard it dug against the zipper of my slacks.

She bent over, her chest on the floor, her ass in the air. She knew what I liked to see, knew what to do. Sofie fucking wanted this too, needed it as much as I did. Giving herself to me, submitting. Where she had control in all other aspects of her life, in this one moment, with me, I was in control. I was the one calling the shots, making her decisions.

"Spread your legs wider, let me see those pretty little pink lips." She did what I said so fucking nicely, so obediently. And when she was in position, I forced myself not to reach down and touch myself. I needed to prolong this, needed to make this last, or I'd come before it even started. "Look at that," I said deeply. "So fucking ready for me. So damn perfect."

I watched as she took a deep breath, maybe steadying herself, maybe trying to control her emotions. She lowered her upper body to the floor so now her breasts were touching the no doubt cold tile. Her ass was popped out in the air, obscenely displayed for my viewing pleasure.

And like a good girl, she waited for the next command.

I let her stay in that position for long seconds and then cleared my throat. "Turn around and face me, but stay on your hands and knees."

When she was in the position I wanted, our gazes locked, my cock so fucking hard it was physically painful, only then did I allow myself the pleasure of reaching down and adjusting myself. The fucker dug against my zipper, as if trying to bust through the damn thing.

"Crawl to me." I made no apologies for who I was or what I liked. This was me. This was how I was with Sofie. Only her. "I said crawl to me. Don't make me ask again." But this was what she needed, what we both needed. I was in command, and she listened.

I watched as she took a steadying breath and started to move toward me. The closer she got, the more I wanted her. I started undoing my belt then went for the zipper of my slacks. While staring right in her eyes, I grabbed my cock out through only the flap, not even bothering to undo the button, and started stroking myself from root to tip. She was only a foot from me now, still on her hands and knees, and looking so damn delicious I could have gotten off from the sight alone.

"How do you feel right now, baby?" I was trying to control my voice, to not show her I was right on the verge of losing it. "What do you feel like?" I watched as her throat worked when she swallowed.

"I feel cheap," she whispered, and I grinned.

"But you fucking like that, don't you." I didn't pose it like a question.

She nodded.

"Yeah, you fucking like it."

She licked her lips.

I held my dick in my hands, pointing it at her face. She rose up on her knees. "Open that pretty little mouth of yours and suck my cock." She looked down at my erection and licked her lips again. "Do what I say now, because you want my dick in your mouth, because you're so damn hungry for it."

When she rose up and braced her hands on my thighs, I held my breath. And then she was leaning forward and opening her mouth.

I reached out and grabbed a chunk of her hair, pulling her forward and down toward my dick. "Put me in your mouth." I felt her lips brush the tip of my cock. "Yeah, that's so fucking good, Sofie." She opened her mouth even wider and took more of me in. I rested my head back and closed my eyes, letting the pleasure wash through me. "That's it. Good girl."

Sofie started licking at the tip, lapping up the pre-cum that spilled from it. I hummed in approval, my balls drawing up as my orgasm threatened to end this before it really started.

"Tell me how it tastes," I demanded.

"Good," she murmured against me. "Salty."

It turned me the fuck on to hear her say this shit.

She flattened her tongue and ran it along the underside of my length, right up the thick vein beneath the skin.

"More, baby girl," I whispered harshly. "I want you to take all of me in until the tip hits the back of your throat and you fucking gag from it." She moaned after I said that.

She started sucking me with fervor, grabbing the root of my shaft with her hand and stroking it in time with her mouth.

"That's it. Make me come." I still had my hand in her hair and kept her head stationary as she sucked me harder and faster. I started lifting my hips in time with her movements, shoving my cock between her lips, loving how the tip hit the back of her throat. The sound of her gagging nearly had me unloading inside her mouth.

I opened my eyes and lifted my head, staring down at her, turned on by the sight. "Fuck, you look so hot with my cock in your mouth." I started thrusting in time with her bobbing head and increased my speed. "*Christ*. That's so fucking it."

I couldn't hold off, not at this rate. I started breathing heavier and tightened my hold on her hair. She hummed around my length, and a deep groan left me.

"Fuck," I growled, knowing I couldn't stop the orgasm from rising. I just let it happen, let the pleasure wash through me. I pushed her head down, letting my cock be completely engulfed in her mouth, and only then did I let off my load.

I made her swallow all my cum, made her take every last drop. When I was semi-hard, I pulled her off my shaft and stared at her mouth. Her lips were red and swollen, glossy. And the sight of a little drop of my jizz at the corner of her mouth had my dick getting hard all over again. I reached out and wiped off the drop before pressing the digit to the seam of her lips. "Clean it off."

And when she opened for me and licked my finger clean, I thought I'd come again right then. She had this wicked way to her, one that had me losing all self-control, all rationalization. When I was with her, all I wanted to do was fuck her until she couldn't walk straight, until all she thought about when she moved was how sore her pussy was because I'd pounded the hell out of her sweet spot.

I was standing and had her off the floor and in my arms a second later. With my hand cupping her nape, urging her to tilt her head back to look at me, I stared at her lips.

"I hope you're ready," I whispered.

"Ready for what?"

Oh, she knew, but she was playing this innocent little thing right now.

I smirked. "Ready to get fucked."

Because we were just getting started.

CHAPTER THIRTEEN

Jareth

I had her in my room before she could utter a word, and then I leaned in and captured her mouth with mine, grabbed the back of her head, tangling her hair in my hand, and kissed her until she was breathless.

I ground my hard cock against her belly. "You feel that?" I murmured against her lips. "You see what you do to me? Getting me off then making me hard all over again?"

She nodded, and I took hold of her upper arms, pulling her away from me, looking down at her naked body, and groaning like a feral animal.

Right now, I loomed over her, my body all

muscle and masculinity, her a little petite female who was about to get devoured by me. I lifted my gaze over her breasts and along her puckered nipples, finally settling on her mouth. She licked her lips, and I held in my groan at the sight. I started walking forward, causing her to move backward, until the mattress stopped her from moving anymore. And then I gently pushed her down. She sat on the bed and looked up at me, her dark hair framed around her face, her big blue eyes wide and trusting.

"Lean back." My voice was dark and almost foreboding.

She placed her hands behind her and leaned slightly back. The position had her breasts thrusting out, and my mouth watered. I leaned down so my mouth was an inch away from hers. Our breathing mingled, coexisted, and my arousal increased. I could feel her need for me as if it was my own.

"Tell me what I want to hear." I was being a sadistic bastard right now, but I needed to hear the words come from her. "Go on, Sofie. Tell me what I want to hear." My voice was low and strained, and I was having a hard time even getting the words out.

She took a deep, steadying breath before she spoke. "Fuck me. Fuck me hard, like I like."

I let a slow grin spread across my mouth. Satisfaction filled me, and my cock jerked in response to her words.

I straightened, keeping my focus on her, and started taking my clothes off. Once my shirt was off and tossed to the side, I went for my pants, never taking my gaze from her, never letting it waver.

And then I was getting on the bed, climbing over her, and forcing Sofie to lean all the way back. She moaned when I placed my weight fully on her, letting her body sink into the mattress, letting her know who was the stronger one here.

I held the side of her face and stroked my thumb along her cheek, just staring into her face, marveling that she was here, that she was mine. "Touch me," I said softly, breaking out of the hardened dominant role and just needing to feel her touch. She grounded me, stabilized everything that I was.

She brought her arms up and wound them around my neck, her upper body rising up slightly and her breasts pressing to my chest.

I moved my other hand over her hip and down her thigh, softly squeezing her flesh. My body, my skin... hell, the very marrow in my bones was alive with pleasure, and it was all because of Sofie.

When I moved my hand inward, so close to her

pussy, I felt her tremble underneath me. "You like that?" I asked softly.

"Yes."

Trying not to go full-on caveman on her was a hard fucking job. I moved my fingers over her pussy, her slick heat causing every muscle in my body to tighten in response.

"You know why we fit together so well?" My voice had gotten harder, and I let my fingers smooth up and down her slit.

"Because I'm soft to your hard," she responded instantly.

We both knew this wasn't in a literal sense. She needed my dominance like I needed her submission. But this wasn't just about us fucking. Before her, I'd kept myself celibate, focusing on building my career, my empire. Then she came along, and I knew she was the one for me.

She was *The One*.

"That's right, baby." My voice was husky and had an edge of unrestrained aggression laced through it. We both needed this.

Give it to her.

"I want you," she begged.

"Shhh, baby girl. You don't ask. I give. Understand?"

She nodded and closed her eyes, moaning softly, a nonverbal plea for more.

"Look at me, Sofie." When she was looking at me once more, I moved my finger up to her clit and started rubbing slow circles around the bundle of nerves. "Wider. Spread your legs wider for me."

Her chest was rising and falling frantically, but she did what I said. When I looked down, I saw her nipples were tight, hard. The areolas were a deep pink, her arousal evident right under her skin.

"Surrender to me," I groaned and leaned down to kiss and lick at her throat. "Put your hands above your head." Once she obeyed, I leaned back and just stared down at her. She was like an offering.

My offering.

I reached out and used my thumbs to gently pull her pussy lips apart until they were stretched wide. And then I was moving lower, blowing a stream of hot breath along the most intimate part of her, loving how she shook for me because of it.

I kissed her inner thighs, ran my tongue over her skin, and loved how she clenched her hands in the sheets. "I fucking love you, Sofie. I love you enough to share you." I don't why I said that, but the words were already out before I could even try and censor them.

She gasped, and I didn't know if it was from my touch or my words.

"Say you love me. Say it." I added pressure to her inner thighs, my hands like vices on her flesh.

"I love you." Those words were nothing but a little breathy moan from her.

She made a small noise for me, and I wafted another stream of warm breath over her perfect pussy. She arched her neck when I ran my tongue up her slit.

"Please."

"Please what, baby?" I kept moving my tongue up and down her center but had my focus trained right on her face, watching her expressions, seeing her pleasure.

"Fuck me already."

I growled low. "You don't give the orders, Sofie. I do. You know that, baby girl."

She thrashed her head back and forth. "I know, but I ache for you, Jareth."

Fuck.

Every muscle in my body was strung tight, ready to explode. When I ran my tongue along her pussy hole, drawing circles, she gasped. And when I pushed the muscle into her, Sofie's back arched and she cried out.

"Like that? Is this how you want it?"

"Yes," she moaned. "God, yes, Jareth."

While fucking her with my tongue, I rubbed my finger back and forth over her clit. I licked and sucked on her, and then moved my mouth to her clit. The flavor of her exploded on my tongue, making me hungry for more. I sucked on her, humming around that tiny bundle of nerves until she arched even more for me, thrusting her breasts out.

"Look what I'm doing to you," I murmured against her pussy. When she lifted her upper body up and looked down the length of her, I growled low in appreciation.

I leaned only an inch back, just enough so that she could fully see what I was doing to her. And then I stuck my tongue out and moved it in small circles around her clit, my gaze never leaving her. I licked at her like she was a fucking ice cream cone on a hot July day and there was no way I was going to lose one drop.

Moving my tongue lower, I teased her pussy hole right before thrusting inside her. She parted her lips on a soft moan, and I felt her open her thighs even wider, letting me in even more.

"Do you want to know how you taste?" My words were muffled against her slick, smooth flesh. I didn't wait for her to respond. "You taste like fucking vanilla and honey, like my future and everything I call mine, Sofie." I could have eaten her out all fucking night, but instead I gave her pussy one last lick and moved up the length of her body, kissing every inch I could reach until I got to her mouth.

I forced my tongue in her mouth, making her taste herself, making her take everything. She moaned when I began a slow grind against her, and the hard, aching length of my cock pressed right between her slit.

"Go on, baby girl," I murmured against her mouth. "Rub that sweet little pussy on me."

When she started lifting her hips and thrusting her cunt against my length, I could have lost it right then and there.

Our rhythm became tandem, and as the seconds ticked by, our kiss deepened, and the grinding pressure increased until I had to break the kiss and inhale sharply. I buried my face in the crook of her neck and started pumping my dick against her harder and faster.

Sliding my hands up her arms, I circled my fingers around her wrists, holding her arms to the mattress as I found a rhythm that had us both groaning.

She gasped when I thrust my cock especially hard against her. She was fueling the fire inside me, teasing me to the very brink without even doing anything more than taking what I had to give her.

I had my lips on her neck, licking and nipping at her flesh, all the while continuing to pump against her. She was saturated for me, so wet I could feel her juices covering my shaft and making a perfect lube for my thrusting.

I'd have no fucking trouble shoving my dick in her; that was for sure.

She started lifting her hips slightly, pushing against me. Identical moans left both of us.

"Please, Jareth. Please. Fuck me." The breathy moans spilling from her had my cock growing impossibly harder. "I *need* you to be inside me."

I let out a muffled sound of pleasure and reached between our bodies to take hold of my cock and place the tip at her entrance. The bulbous head pushed at her hole, wanting in, needing to feel that strangulating hold she'd have over him.

I knew she'd come for me soon. I could feel it, practically taste it. There was no more waiting, not just for her, but for my own sanity. I thrust the head inside her and leaned back enough to look down at where we were joined. She lifted her hips and arched her back, and I pushed another couple inches into her giving, hot, and tight pussy.

My hands were on her hips now, holding her stationary as I sank into her inch by slow, agonizingly slow inch.

And when my balls were flush with her round ass, I groaned and stilled my movements. She panted, her breasts shaking slightly as she held her hands above her head like a good girl.

Looking back down at where we were conjoined, I reached out, pressed my thumb against her clit, and ran small circles along the swollen little bud. She kept shifting beneath me, trying to get some friction. I rested one hand on her waist, soothing her.

"I'm in control," I reminded her, and she stilled. I started slowly pulling out of her then, knowing it teased and tormented her. "Touch me." I needed to have her hands on me while I claimed her.

Sofie curled her fingers around my forearm, her other hand on her breast, tweaking at the nipple as she watched me.

And then when just the tip was at her entrance, I shoved back in hard.

"Yes," she cried out and ached her neck, her eyes closed and her nails digging into my arm.

"Open your eyes and look at me when I get you off."

And just as she looked at me, I felt her pussy clamp down on my dick as she came.

I growled low and started fucking her then, slamming into her and pulling back out. Over and over. Faster and harder.

The sounds of sloppy, hot sex filled the bedroom.

Her cheeks were pink, her pupils dilated, and her breathing erratic as she came for me.

"You are so fucking beautiful when you get off for me."

"Jareth." She cried out my name as she threw her head back and clearly rode out the pleasure.

I watched her breath catch as her orgasm peaked, and I inhaled sharply, the sight such a turn-on there was no way I could hold off.

The pleasure-filled tremors were never ending in their onslaught as another climax peaked inside her, and then exploded like a thousand tiny pieces of glass.

"Seeing you like this, so fucking unhinged because of me, makes me want to fill you with my cum." My voice was strangled, and I gritted my teeth, wanting her to be completely sated before I found my own release.

"Then do it. Fill me up."

I cursed after she said that.

My hands were on either side of her head as I slammed into her and retreated.

Slammed into her and retreated.

I did the same motions over and over again, sweat dripping from my hairline and chest and landing on her breasts. The full, heavy weight of my balls slapped against her ass repeatedly when I pounded into her. I grabbed her calf and lifted it over my shoulder, and then leaned back slightly. My focus was on where our bodies were joined once more.

"I love seeing my cock going into your sweet little pussy. This is mine." I pushed the remaining inches into her and pulled back out. I did this with measured, steady movements. My focus was on her the entire time. I couldn't tear my gaze from Sofie, even if I'd wanted to. Head downcast, gaze trained right on her, and this feeling of being drugged consuming me, I knew I might look insane.

With my arms braced on either side of her and my muscles strained, there was no way I could control myself anymore.

She pushed herself up and looked down at where I fucked her, a gasp-moan leaving her at the sight. I watched my cock tunnel in and out of her pussy hole. She was stretched wide around my length. I moved faster into her, pulling out and pumping back in. The sound of our wet skin slapping together filled the room, driving my need higher.

"Perfectly made for me," I said to myself, my voice cracking on the end as ecstasy stole my sanity, a telling sign that I was about to go over the edge.

"I'm so close again, Jareth."

I grunted. "You going to come again for me, baby?"

She nodded and fell back on the bed, her hands going to her hair as she tugged at the strands.

I moved my thumb to her clit and started rubbing it again quickly. The sound of her pussy suctioning my dick was an auditory orgasm.

So close. So. Fucking. Close.

And then she opened her mouth to cry out her second climax herself. Her pussy tightened around my cock, milking it until I was lost in... her.

My breathing hitched, and I pulled out of her, grabbing my cock and stroking the fucker as my orgasm rushed to the surface. Her pussy juices soaked my length, and I used it as lube to jerk myself off. Although the idea of filling her up with my cum was tempting, I loved seeing my seed covering her pretty peach skin.

The tightening at the base of my spine increased and then I felt it explode out of me. I opened my eyes and stared down at her, seeing ribbon after ribbon of cum shoot out of me and land on her belly and breasts. She had her mouth parted as she let me paint her, as she took it all.

When I was spent dry, I collapsed next to her and breathed out harshly. "You fucking wear me out, baby."

She chuckled softly beside me and rolled, pressing her chest to the side of my body, the feeling of her damp skin another turn-on.

Mine. Yeah, she was mine.

CHAPTER FOURTEEN

Sofie

"So, this is really last minute, but are you free this weekend, like Sunday?" It was technically my "free day," which was why I'd picked it, so it didn't interfere with my time with the guys.

"For you, I'd drop everything and anything." He shifted on the bed and cupped my cheek, looking into my eyes. "You know that. You tell me when and where, and I'm there no matter what."

I couldn't help the heat that rose to my cheeks at his words. God, he was so devoted to me.

I thought about how we lay there, me pressed against Jareth's body, his arm around my shoulders, his fingers moving up and down my arm. I had goose bumps from his touch, and the silence that stretched between us was comfortable... comforting.

"My mom is coming over with her new boyfriend, and Ryker is coming." I looked at his face for any sign of how he'd take that, but all he did was smile softly and continue to tickle my arm.

He then leaned closer and kissed me on the forehead. "Whatever you want, baby." His voice was rough, coarse.

We lay there in silence again, and I listened to the steady beat of his heart right under my ear.

"Does it bother you?" he asked after several comfortable, silent moments had passed.

"Does what bother me?" I rose up slightly so I could give him my full attention.

He stared into my eyes, and I got lost in his dark brown ones. They were like melted chocolate, smooth and delicious.

"Does it bother you that I'm so much older than you?"

I shook my head instantly. "No. I don't even think about it." And that was the honest truth. Although he was old enough to be my father, had experienced and accomplished so much by the time he'd been my age, I just saw him as Jareth, the man I loved.

"I worry sometimes that being with me may complicate things even more." He smoothed his finger along my cheek. "But I'm too selfish to walk away."

My chest hurt at the very thought of losing him. "Good, because I'm too selfish to let you go either." He gently pulled me down again so I was lying on his chest once more. "Does it bother you I'm with Ryker too?" I supposed if we were spilling it all I might as well ask him.

Long moments of silence stretched out, but he didn't feel tense, and I didn't feel any kind of anger coming from him. He just held me, running his fingers along my skin, relaxing me further.

"Jareth?"

He finally shook his head slowly. "The thought of you with any other man infuriates me, has this protective rage filling me. I want to kill any motherfucker who even looks at you, Sofie, who even thinks he can talk to you."

I stared into his warm brown eyes.

"But then I think about you with Ryker, and as crazy as it all is, I don't feel any of that jealous rage. I know he'll protect you, take care of you. Just as much as I will. Just as strongly as I will. That calms me, makes me feel secure that you'll always be looked after." He lifted his hand up and stroked it along the side of my head, picking up a strand of my hair and running it between his fingers. "It's fucking insane, isn't it?"

I smiled softly and shook my head. "No, I think it's exactly how things are supposed to work out. I think that's why things are so easy and fluid between the three of us. It's fate, and as cheesy and corny as that may sound, I really believe we are all meant to be together."

"Do you know how much I love you, Sofie?"

I let my fingers trail across his stomach, his six-pack flexing under my touch. "Probably as much as I love you," I teased back affectionately.

He shifted so he could look at me again, tilting my head back and staring at my face.

"I love you," I said again. He was one of the great loves of my life.

Ryker was the other.

I rested my head on his chest and closed my eyes. I had no idea how I'd gotten so lucky, how things had just seemed to fall into place.

Here's to having everything else fall into place this easily.

CHAPTER FIFTEEN

Sofie

The night of the dinner

I wiped my hands on my apron. I was running behind, and I probably could've ordered carry-out for tonight, maybe even should have so I wasn't running around like a chicken with my head cut off. Although my mom had offered to cook her special pasta dish, I insisted on being the one to treat her to a home-cooked meal. I wanted everything to be perfect and special.

I looked over at the table, having rented a large banquet-sized one for everyone because the two-seater one we had in the kitchen was not even close to fitting all of us.

A white linen tablecloth covered it, teal and white place settings perfectly situated. I'd bought them months ago and was just now getting around to using them. But I supposed now was the perfect situation to put them to good use. I'd even had to go out and buy actual silverware, because the mismatched shit we had and the random plastic takeout sporks weren't going to cut it.

I checked on the lasagna, keeping it warm in the oven. The house smelled of Italian seasonings and garlic bread. With a salad sitting in the center of the table, Parmesan cheese, croutons, and olive oil and red wine vinegar as a dressing sitting beside that, I felt a smile play across my face.

"Not bad, Sofie. Not bad at all."

The red wine was chilling in the fridge, as well as the strawberry and blueberry parfait I'd whipped up real quick. I'd paid close attention to details, because I felt like tonight was a make or break situation. I didn't know why I felt like that. It was like I was going for my first job interview, or maybe going to prom. I didn't think I'd ever been so nervous in my entire life.

I took off the apron and carried it to my bedroom, tossing it in the hamper and checking my appearance in the mirror that hung on the back of my door. Everyone would be here soon, and after I wiped a splatter of marinara sauce off my cheek, touched up my nude lipstick, and ran my fingers through my hair, I exhaled and told myself this was as good as it was going to get.

Just then, I heard car doors closing, and my heart jumped to my throat. "Here we go," I whispered.

I walked toward the living room and pulled the curtain aside, looking outside. Jareth's sleek black luxury car sat in the driveway, and right beside that was Ryker's Tahoe. The two men were looking at each other, and although maybe to an outsider it might seem as if they were sizing each other up, I knew better.

They were mature about all of this, accepting.

Jareth walked around the front of Ryker's vehicle and held his hand out. They were both manly-men, alphas. They were the same but so, so different.

And I knew that's why I'd fallen in love with both of them.

The longer I stared at them, the more I realized they both made my heart race, my palms sweat, and had me wishing we could just fly out to some private island where no one could hurt us with their words, looks, or judgment.

They both finally started heading toward the

front door, and I opened it before they could knock. Before any of us could say anything, I saw a white Jeep Wrangler pull up to the curb in front of the house. The windows were too tinted for me to see who the driver was, but I knew it was my mother and her new boyfriend.

I turned my attention back to Ryker and Jareth. Ryker was in front of me first, and he didn't hesitate in curling his hand around my neck and pulling me in for a kiss. It was a slow-burn one, passionate and consuming. I melted against him and moaned, my body heating up passionately.

He broke away far too soon, and a small sound of disappointment left me. But Jareth was stepping forward right away, stealing his hand around my waist, and pulling me flush against his hard body.

He kissed me just as intensely, claiming me just as fully as Ryker had. I actually curled my fingers around the frame of the door to steady myself.

When Jareth pulled away, I sucked in a lungful of air, feeling lightheaded. My heart was racing as I realized both of them were staring at me as if they were barely holding on to their control. Heavy-lidded expressions, pupils dilated, the start of tented pants.

Yeah, if they hadn't stopped, we'd be in my room fucking right now, no doubt.

The sound of car doors closing had me remembering the Jeep. I saw my mom walking toward us, a man behind her but shielded by her form so I couldn't quite make him out.

My mom lifted her hand and waved enthusiastically. I'd never seen her have such a glow on her face before, had never seen her smile so wide. She looked beautiful, with her hair all done up and her formfitting dress showing off her curves.

I waved, still trying to see the man behind her. When she was right next to us, Jareth and Ryker both turned to face her. She was about as tall as I was, so she had to crane her neck back to look into their faces.

First, she eyed Jareth up and down then turned her focus to Ryker. This was the first time she was meeting Jareth, and I could see that although she was a little curious meeting him while Ryker was here too, there was no condemnation coming from her.

She wrapped her arms around Jareth and gave him a big bear hug, and I stifled a laugh when I saw how big his eyes got. He looked stiff, unsure. He probably didn't know what the hell to do.

"I won't bite," she said with a grin and pulled back.

"Not unless you ask for it." The teasing sound of a man's voice reminded me she wasn't alone. As she gave Ryker a hug, I turned my focus to the guy she'd come with.

I felt my eyes widen as I got a good look at him. He was my age, young and attractive, and had this cocky expression on his face. My mom stepped back, and her new beau wrapped his arm around her waist, pulling her in close to him.

"Sofie," she said, "I'd like you to meet Trevor, the guy I've been seeing for the past two months."

Trevor grinned and held his hand out for me to shake. I took a step forward, and Ryker and Jareth both did the same, flanking me as if they were worried about me touching Trevor. I shook my head and smiled, taking Trevor's hand and shaking it.

"I can see where Theresa gets her good looks from," Trevor said.

Jareth and Ryker both made a low, disapproving sound.

"Don't worry about them," I said and let go of his hand. "Their bark is worse than their bite."

Jareth grunted, and Ryker snorted.

And then there was a moment of awkward

silence with everyone just staring at each other. "Well, should we go inside and eat?" I finally asked to break up the weird situation that suddenly fell over us.

My mother smiled, and I saw her reach down to take Trevor's hand in hers. "We plan on going bar hopping tonight, and Trevor rented a swanky hotel room overlooking the city."

I really didn't want to hear about my mom getting drunk, staying with her boyfriend at a hotel, and doing... not sleeping.

I could see she was happy with him, could tell that from the way she looked at him. It was nice seeing her genuinely smile. And it looked like Trevor was just as smitten with her too, if the wink he gave her and the way he leaned in to kiss her cheek were anything to go by.

We headed inside, and I could hear my mom giggling behind us. I looked over my shoulder and saw Trevor whispering something in her ear.

"You're so bad," she said softly, but not too softly that we all hadn't heard. She was also blushing, which made me image what Trevor had just said to her.

And as we headed inside, all I could think was I

hoped tonight didn't end up getting someone's ass kicked.

"For real?" Trevor looked between Jareth, Ryker, and myself, his eyes wide. My mother, on the other hand, who sat beside him, looked apologetic, embarrassed, but amused. "That's wild," Trevor said as he looked between the three of us. He took another swig from his wineglass. "So you are all a throuple? Or do they call it a threesome now?" He picked up his wine glass and took a long drink. "It's like Jerry Springer," he added after setting his glass down. "Or that one show where the guy has all those wives, but it's reversed." Trevor started laughing. He reached for the wine bottle to fill his glass for the fourth time.

"I think maybe you've had enough," my mom said a little uneasily.

He shook his head and looked at my mother. "I'm good, Theresa."

My mom exhaled wearily.

"So, like... how does it work?" he asked, and the table stayed silent.

I could feel the anger coming from Jareth and

Ryker, who sat on either side of me. I knew they were getting to their breaking point with Trevor. I think we all were. I felt possessive anger practically spilling from them.

"Like, do you guys swap off every other day? Do y'all just sleep in one big California king bed? Details. Give us some details." Trevor downed half his wine glass before setting the cup down and hiccupping.

"Trevor, it's very inappropriate to be asking my daughter those questions," my mom said in a stern voice. She glanced at me, and I shook my head, silently telling her, *"It's okay, not your fault."*

I didn't expect anyone to be okay with my relationship, or even understand it. I didn't even care what anyone thought about it. But I did expect respect, especially in my own house.

And I was about to say that when I felt Jareth become tense beside me.

"You'll do well to watch your mouth, *son*." Jareth said those words so low, so deep, that even I felt chills move along my body. He had his hands on top of the table, his fingers curled toward his palms so they were in tight fists, his knuckles white.

I glanced over at him and swallowed roughly,

could see how enraged he was right now as he stared at Trevor.

"Son?" Trevor started to chuckle and looked at my mother. When he looked back at us, he had a glassy-eyed expression on his face.

"Maybe you've had enough wine," I said softly, trying to keep my tone easygoing. I wasn't his mother, but he was going over the line.

And because he'd been drinking so much, it was clear his loose lips were going to get him in trouble.

"I can hold my alcohol," he replied with a slur in his voice and grinned at me, almost challenging me to test him in his admission. He looked back at Jareth. "I guess I am young enough to be your son... and hers." Trevor started chuckling again and glanced at me. "Tell me, Sofie," Trevor prompted and leaned forward, his voice lowering as if he were about to tell me a secret. "Which one do you like better? Which one really knows how to push your buttons... if you know what I mean?" He wagged his eyebrows up and down and grinned.

"That's enough, Trevor," my mom said again, her anger clear. "You'll respect my daughter and her guests."

I heard a low, rough sound leave Ryker. I snapped my head toward him, felt my eyes widen as he slowly pushed himself out of the chair, his massive six-foot-four frame straightening as he commanded the entire room.

"Not only are you disrespecting the woman we love, but you're disrespecting and embarrassing the woman right next to you."

I watched as Trevor swallowed, the realization of how he'd ruined dinner clear on his face.

"I think it's time we leave," my mother said and gave me an apologetic and sad smile.

"You don't have to go," I said and stood when my mother did.

"Honey, I think it's best. Trevor needs to go, and I'm not going to let him drive to the hotel in his condition."

Trevor stood and his cheeks were flushed, as no doubt embarrassment flooded him. "I'm sorry," he muttered. He left the kitchen, and we stood there in silence.

"I can take him to the hotel if you're not comfortable doing it," both Jareth and Ryker seemed to say at the same time.

"No, no. I'm fine. And he'll be fine once he sobers up." My mom stared at Trevor as he headed toward the front door. "The young ones always like to live life to the fullest." She sighed and glanced back at us. "Maybe that's why I'm so drawn to him, because he makes me feel young again, and it's been a long time since I felt that way."

"I get it, but if he treats you like shit, Mom—"

"He doesn't, honey. He's got a big mouth, but that's where it ends. Believe me, no man is going to put me down."

I smiled, because I knew my mom was one tough cookie.

"But I'm really sorry, sweetheart. I didn't mean to ruin the night and embarrass everyone."

I shook my head. "You didn't, Mom. It's fine. Wine gets to my head too, and it's not like I expected him to understand this situation fully after just meeting us. It takes some getting used to."

"He was disrespectful," Jareth said.

"I was about ready to pop him in the jaw," Ryker inserted next, and I gave him a small smile, knowing both of them meant well.

The next thing I knew, Trevor was walking back toward us with this sheepish look on his face. "Listen, I wanted to apologize. I should've kept my mouth shut. It's not my business about any of this. I guess I let the wine, my ego, and curiosity get the best of me." He ran his hands down his Dockers, his nerves evident. "I really am sorry though."

I could tell he was being genuine, knew he was embarrassed. "It's fine. It's done and over with." And I meant that. "Just don't let it become a habit, especially with my mother," I said seriously, fiercely protective of my mom.

I didn't want anything sour between us, especially if my mom did care for him. He turned and left, and my mom hugged all three of us before following him to the front door. Once I heard it shut, I walked toward the living room window and pulled the curtain aside, watching as they headed toward his Jeep.

But before she got in the vehicle, I could see her start to give him an earful, pointing to the house and shaking her head. I could just imagine what she was saying, how she was putting him in his place about being respectful. My mother didn't lack the ability to make someone know and understand that what they'd done was absolutely unacceptable.

"He's lucky we didn't beat his fucking ass," Ryker said.

"I was two seconds away from slapping the fucking curiosity out of him," Jareth agreed.

I snorted and shook my head. "You guys are so big and bad, aren't you?" Before I knew what was going on, Jareth had his arm wrapped around my shoulders, and Ryker curled his fingers around my waist. I was sandwiched between them, warmth filling me, contentment making me feel whole.

"She looks happy though, right?" I was speaking more to myself than to anyone else, but I felt my guys tighten their hold on me slightly.

"That she does," Ryker murmured.

"He better treat her well," Jareth said.

Ryker grunted in agreement. "Or I see an ass-whooping in his future."

I looked between my two boys and knew that things would work out. I could feel it.

CHAPTER SIXTEEN

Sofie

Later that evening.

I was snuggled against Ryker's chest, my legs sprawled over Jareth's lap as he lazily massaged my bare feet, his touch relaxing, warming. Ryker had his arm around my shoulders, his fingers curled around my bicep.

My mother and Trevor had left hours ago, and after we all cleaned up, Ryker had run down to the ice cream shop and brought us back a giant, three-person hot fudge sundae that we devoured, laughing as we finished off another bottle of wine. Now we found ourselves lazily watching a comedy. Having my guys on either side of me felt so right. All of us playing house felt like we should have done it ages ago.

That's how it felt to me, at least. Did it feel that way for them as well?

I knew what I wanted to talk about, and what better time than right now as I sat between Ryker and Jareth? I was nervous and scared of their response, their reaction. But if I didn't do this now, I'd never know.

"Can I talk to you guys?" There was this shift in the atmosphere, the room seeming to still, the air growing thick. Seriousness surrounded us.

"Absolutely, Sofie." Ryker was the one to speak first.

"You have our full attention always, baby girl," Jareth said next.

God, why couldn't I breathe? Why was the room so hot? Why did it feel like it was closing in on me?

I pushed myself off the couch and walked a few steps away from them, turning so that I could look into their faces when I brought this up. My heart was pounding so hard it was painful, and as Jareth and Ryker stared at me, their full attention trained right on me, I started to question if this was really the best thing for me to do.

But no time like the present, right?

We only live once, and none of us were getting any younger. The worst thing that they could say was no, that it wasn't a good idea. But I wouldn't know unless I asked. Taking that chance was the best thing I could do in this moment. And too much time had already passed without me knowing how our futures would go.

Alone.

Or together.

All of us.

The three of us.

"I wanted to talk about all of us..." I swallowed, a thick lump deciding to take up residence in my throat.

"What is it, baby?" Ryker asked, looking concerned all of a sudden.

"Sofie, you're kind of worrying me, and I'm sure Ryker as well," Jareth said and straightened. Ryker made a deep sound of agreement.

I could do this. I could. I had to.

So I took a deep breath, willed myself to have strength, and just came out and said it. "I love both of you," I said and looked in each of their eyes, making sure they knew I was being serious, that this was coming from the heart. "I love both of you so much. I know us being together is unconventional, but I need you both in my life more than I've ever needed anything else." I took a deep, steadying breath. "If I lost one of you—" The very thought had emotion rising up viciously in me. "—I'd feel like a piece of myself was missing." I tried to sound strong, but I heard the way my voice cracked.

I'd been honest with them individually, and they knew how I felt, but having them both sit there in front of me as I talked about the feelings I had for both of them made me want to spill my entire heart. "I feel this connection with both of you, one that I've never felt before, that I never will feel with anyone else. I know with everything in me that you both were meant to be mine, just as I was meant to be yours."

No one said anything for long seconds, their expressions stoic, their attention trained on me.

"But I understand if this isn't something you guys see for yourself, see for your future. And as much as I love you, as much as I want you, I want you to have that choice. I understand if this is too complicated, if a monogamous relationship is what you're after." God, could they hear how fast and hard my heart was beating? "But what I want is both of you. And I know you said you're okay with that. But are you really?" A suspended moment passed, and I waited for one of them—both of them—to respond.

Ryker cleared his throat, and Jareth shifted on the couch.

"What is it you actually see, Sofie?" Ryker was the one to speak first once again.

I swallowed. "I told you. I want both of you."

He shook his head slowly. "No, I mean what do you really want?"

For a moment, I didn't know what he meant. I'd spilled my heart to them, told them everything. And then as I looked into his eyes, glancing over at Jareth, I knew what he wanted. I knew what they both wanted.

"Tell us, baby girl."

I looked to Jareth after he spoke. Yes, I knew what they wanted to hear. It's what I wanted to say.

"I want all three of us together. I want us sleeping under the same roof, no more days split up between us, no more bouncing back and forth. I don't want a *ménage à trois*." A long pause filled the air. "I want two separate relationships, with the two men I love the most. But I want us all living together. And I want you guys to want that too."

And then more silence, awkwardness filling me as I waited for them to tell me if that's what they wanted too. God, I was on pins and needles. They'd told me many times they didn't care that I was with the other, but what I was telling them, asking them, was far different than what they'd probably bargained for.

A throuple, as Trevor had put it.

A poly relationship.

I wasn't interested in us being together sexually at the same time. I liked how things were now, and I suspected they did as well. And I tried not to dwell on the idea that they'd tell me they didn't want that, that they'd been thinking about this arrangement and it wasn't what they wanted after all.

And then Ryker was the first to stand. He walked over to me but didn't touch me, and I held my breath as I tipped my head back and looked into his face.

"Say something. Anything," I whispered.

"Sofie." He said my name so softly I wondered if I had really heard him say it. "I've known you my entire life. I've loved you for nearly as long." He paused a moment, and I could see on his face he was gathering his thoughts. "The only thing I ever wanted was to make you happy." He reached out and cupped my cheek then, smoothing his thumb right under my eyes. "There is no me without you. There is no life if you're not in it." He took a step closer to me. "I'm man enough, secure in my masculinity and our love for each other, to know that you need Jareth. I know he's not a replacement for me, but an extension of what you need."

I didn't want to cry, but Ryker was saying things I felt so deeply I was on the verge of doing just that.

"So, my point is, I'm not going anywhere, baby. You're stuck with me for life, and that's all I've ever wanted." He leaned down and kissed me, and I rose on my toes to meet him, wrapping my arms around his neck and letting him pull me in close. After a long moment, he pulled back and smiled. "Besides, Jareth isn't so bad," he said and winked, looking over his shoulder and staring at the other man I was hopelessly in love with.

Ryker pulled back and stepped away, moving to stand by the back of the couch, letting Jareth take his place.

Jareth rose and moved toward me. He wasn't in the three-piece suit I normally saw him in, but instead wore a pair of jeans and a button-down shirt. He had this intense expression on his face, something I was used to seeing, something that always made my heart race.

He was only a foot from me, looking down into my eyes, both of us sharing the same air. Although I hadn't known him as long as I had Ryker, and although I hadn't given my virginity to him like I had with the man who stood just a few feet from him, I'd given a different part of myself to him.

I'd submitted to him fully, opened my heart to him completely.

We shared something special as well. He'd given me experiences that I never thought possible. He gave me things Ryker hadn't, and vice versa. And that's how I knew we were all supposed to be together, all made for each other.

But I held my breath, waiting for him to speak.

"Sofie," he said softly, and I held my breath. "So many things were said tonight," he continued in a deep, husky voice. "So many things I knew, so many things I didn't know." He lifted his dark gaze and looked at my face. "My blue-eyed angel." His voice was nothing more than a deep growl. "The only thing I want for you is to be happy, to live your life the way you want." I saw emotion on his face. "And I'm lucky enough to be part of that future you want. We both are." He lifted his hand and pushed some hair away from my cheek, letting his fingers play across my temple. "I'm okay with not having you fully. But I'll only be okay with you giving yourself to Ryker. Only ever with him."

I swallowed and looked over his shoulder at where Ryker stood. His hands were curled around the back of the couch, his jaw tight, a muscle ticking beneath the scruff.

"I think it's safe to say that both of us want you badly enough, love you unconditionally enough, that we're willing to share you, Sofie," Ryker said and moved around the couch to stand next to Jareth. He lifted his hand and slid his fingers up my neck, the digits trailing along my pulse point. He cupped one side of my throat while Jareth held the other.

And both of my men looked at me, giving me everything, giving me all they were.

"To be our wife," Jareth said.

"To be the mother of our children." Ryker was the next one to speak.

"To only be ours. Always, Sofie."

They seemed to say that last part in unison, in sync, as if they were thinking the same thing, wanting the same thing.

And then they pulled me in for an embrace, and I inhaled both of their scents. The aroma was strong and masculine, gentle and loving. It was the smell of all mine.

Everything mixed together in perfect harmony, driving deep into my very core, my very soul.

And as they held me, as I let myself fall fully into this headfirst, I knew everything would be okay.

I knew everything was exactly how it was supposed to be.

EPILOGUE ONE

Sofie

Two years later

I sat out in the sunroom, looking at the trees and mountains, breathing in the fresh morning air as it breezed in through the open window.

My eyes were closed as I felt the warmth of the early morning sun washing over me. I only had on a silk bathrobe, the one Jareth had given me for my birthday last year, and a pair of fuzzy slippers Ryker had given me for Christmas.

The sound of birds chirping had me opening my eyes, but all I could see was trees, trees for miles. We'd bought this property two years ago, ten acres in

Washington State. It was private, which is what all three of us wanted, open, and picturesque.

Our house had been custom-built, so grand and big that it held the three of us comfortably. It had a main house in the center and two separate buildings attached to that. From the outside, it looked like one grand, rustic estate, but on the inside, it housed three people, two separate families, three different relationships.

A wife and her two husbands.

Ryker had a section on the right, Jareth on the left. And the center was for all of us, our main living area where we could have dinner together, visit, and a place where I could just be with both of them at the same time.

I looked down at my left hand, my ring finger adorned by two platinum bands. I hadn't wanted diamonds, didn't want flash. So when both Jareth and Ryker proposed, on the same day, at the same time, I'd been so happy to see the simple yet elegant bands they presented.

And the inscription on the inside of each band was personal, from both of them, something I would cherish forever.

I smiled, feeling like I had the world in my very

hands. Who knew a girl like me could have a life like this?

I heard someone approaching and looked over my shoulder to see Ryker come in with a mug in his hand. He gave it to me, and I looked down to see the hot tea and milk. I smiled up at him and brought the cup to my mouth, taking a small sip and closing my eyes, humming at the sweet honey flavor.

He sat down on the chair to my left, and we didn't say anything. We just stared at the gorgeous view. But nothing needed to be said. It was a perfect, wonderful silence.

I took another sip of my tea and then set it down on the coffee table in front of me. I reached out with my hand and took Ryker's, twining our fingers together as I rested back fully. It wasn't too long after that when Jareth came in, a small plate in his hand, a pastry atop that. He had a smile on his face, and I could tell it had nothing to do with me sexually, and everything to do with loving me.

He set my pastry down beside my mug and took up residence in the small plush chair on the opposite side of me. I reached my hand out and took his, holding both my husbands' hands, feeling like the luckiest woman in the world.

But then they let go, skimmed their palms over

my belly, and rested them on the slight swell. I was four months pregnant with our first baby. This was the greatest gift I could ever have—we could ever have. And although I didn't know who the biological father was, it didn't matter. Both of them would love this baby as if it were their own.

Because it was theirs. Blood or not, we were all in this together.

I had my two husbands.

They had me.

And we were going to finally be a family and irrevocably connected.

And although it wasn't perfect all the time, although we had our disagreements, our differences, the one thing we had that would never fade... was each other.

We had our love.

EPILOGUE TWO

Sofie

Ten years later

"Deacon and Victor, you better leave Polly alone or it's no dessert for you after dinner," I shouted at the twins, who, although younger than their sister by two years, tormented her until I knew she was ready to scream.

"Sorry, Momma," the boys said in unison and ran off.

Polly huffed out, but there was a thankful expression in her face.

"Dinner in twenty, sweetheart."

She nodded and went back to tending to the flowers she was planting.

I sat back down and watched the boys run over to the swing set Ryker and Jareth had put together last year. Deacon and Victor, identical twins, both spitting images of Ryker. And Polly, our firstborn, looked exactly like Jareth. Hell, she even had his personality and resting bitch face down to perfection.

Although we'd never done a DNA test, frankly because it didn't matter to us, we all knew who the biological parents were.

But to be honest, we didn't care who their father was by blood. Jareth and Ryker took care of the three of them, loved and cherished them, and protected them with their lives as if there was no doubt they'd fathered them all.

I heard the back door open and looked over my shoulder to see Ryker coming out, a tray in his hands, juice boxes for the boys, and three glasses of lemonade for us and Polly. I smiled as he came over and set it down on the patio table, a light breeze moving by us, the wind ruffling the strands of my hair along my shoulders.

"Sweetheart, come and grab something to drink," Ryker called out to Polly.

She stood and brushed off her knees and then was walking over. Once she was only a foot away,

Ryker wrapped his arm around her shoulders and brought her in for a hug. Then he leaned down and kissed the top of her head.

I smiled again, feeling my heart warm at the sight of the bond they had. Ryker winked at me, and I felt my heart skip a beat.

"Thanks, Daddy." Polly grabbed a glass of lemonade and sat beside me, and I moved some hair away from her face.

"How are the flowers going?" Ryker asked as he sat in the chair beside us.

She tipped the glass back and took a small sip. "Good, surprisingly. Maybe I have this whole green thumb thing down after all."

Ryker and I chuckled.

"Of course you do. You're smart as hell, baby girl," Jareth said from behind us.

Jareth had a beer in one hand as he leaned down and kissed Polly on top of the head. He stood beside her as he stared at the boys. "They're fearless," he said, and we all murmured our agreements.

"Dinner is ready," he said and looked over at me, a possessive glint in his eyes.

I felt warm tendrils of desire move through me, the same feeling I got when Ryker gave me that sexy little wink.

"Polly, can you wrangle the boys inside?"

She looked over at me and nodded. "Wish me luck," she joked, and I patted her knee. As she stood and headed over to the swing set, Deacon and Victor spotting her and play screaming, I could only smile and shake my head.

"You're not thirsty, baby?" Ryker asked.

I looked at the untouched lemonade on the table. My stomach did a little flip and I looked over at him, and then turned my attention to Jareth. Both men were already watching me. And the longer I stayed silent, the more I saw the concern on their faces.

"No, I like lemonade just fine, just not right now." I watched as Jareth's eyebrows knitted in confusion. When I looked at Ryker, he had the same expression going on. I placed my hand on my belly and let a slow smile spread across my face. I looked between the two of them. "You know during my first trimester lemons make me queasy." There was a moment of shock I felt come from them, but then I watched as their faces lit up with happiness.

"You're not fucking with us, are you?" Ryker asked, surprise in his voice, but he was grinning from ear to ear.

I shook my head slowly and looked at Jareth.

"Sofie? You're...." He lowered his eyes to my belly, where my hand still rested.

I nodded again. "I haven't gone to the doctor yet, but the three pregnancy tests I took all said I'm pregnant." I felt my cheeks hurt from how wide my smile was. "I'm guessing no more than six weeks along though." Before I knew what was happening, I was pulled up from the chair and into Ryker's arms. He covered my face with kisses, murmuring how happy he was.

Jareth pulled me away from Ryker, and then I was in his arms, his hands cupping my cheeks, his lips on mine. The scent of both of them speared into me.

"Another little one," Jareth said against my mouth.

Although it wasn't like we were actively trying, we also hadn't been using any protection.

Jareth gave me one more lingering kiss before pulling back. Ryker was there to take his place, kissing me, devouring my mouth, and after a moment pulling away to smile from happiness.

"Another baby." He rested his forehead against mine, and at the same time, I felt Jareth rub slow circles along my lower back.

I had both my hands on my belly now and looked down. "Pretty crazy, huh?"

"Not crazy, but fucking perfect," Ryker said.

"God, baby," Jareth murmured. "It's incredible." He took my hand and twined his fingers through mine, giving me a squeeze.

"We should tell the kids tonight," Ryker added softly, and I nodded. Although maybe we should have waited until I was further along, I was too excited about this, and I could tell the guys were as well.

Ryker took my other hand, holding it tightly, and then we turned and looked at our three children. Polly was running from the boys and laughing as they chased her around the swing set. A feeling of perfection and gratitude surrounded me.

I looked up and between Ryker and Jareth, feeling my perpetual smile. Through the ups and downs over the years, through all the wonderful things that happened in our lives, these two men beside me would always have my back. They'd always be in our lives, be our biggest supporters and advocates.

And once again, I couldn't help thinking how I was the luckiest girl in the world.

The End

ALSO BY JENIKA SNOW

SO GOOD

By Jenika Snow

www.JenikaSnow.com

Jenika_Snow@Yahoo.com

Copyright © May 2019 by Jenika Snow

Photographer: Wander Aguiar

Cover Model: Jonny James & Amanda Joan

Image provided by: Wander book club

Cover design by: Designs by Dana

Editor: Kasi Alexander

Content Editor/Proofreader: All Encompassing books

ALL RIGHTS RESERVED: The unauthorized reproduction, transmission, or distribution of any part of this copyrighted work is illegal. Criminal copyright infringement is investigated by the FBI and is punishable by up to five years in federal prison and a fine of $250,000.

This literary work is fiction. Any name, places, characters and incidents are the product of the author's imagination. Any resemblance to actual persons, living or dead, events or establishments is solely coincidental.

Please respect the author and do not participate in or encourage piracy of copyrighted materials that would violate the author's rights.

Matthew

Ivy. So sweet and young, so innocent and mine, even though I was crossing a line by simply desiring her.

Forbidden. I should stay away, but in my mind I'd already claimed her, already made the decision I couldn't let her go.

If wanting her was wrong ... I didn't want to be right.

Ivy

I was still in high school, hadn't even experienced the world, but I already knew who I wanted to spend my life with.

Matthew.

He was someone I could never be with, yet here I was, feeling him, touching him ... being with him. It was all so perfect until it wasn't, until my father found out ... until my world was turned upside down.

And through it all Matthew was there, telling me he wouldn't give me up, wouldn't let me go.

But could he keep that promise during the fallout?

1

Ivy

My very first memories involved Matthew, the way he'd held my hand as he took me to the park. The way he'd helped me on the swing and then pushed me. He'd watched me when my mother and father had been at work, playing board games with me, sneaking hot fudge sundaes before dinner.

He'd been a constant presence in my life always. I trusted him more than anyone else, knew that he'd never let anyone hurt me.

I remember looking up at him, the sun behind him, the glare intense, and thinking he was a superhero.

My superhero.

And when a little boy had been picking on me, Matthew had been there to tell him that treating girls with respect and kindness was the only way to grow up being a good man.

He was Matthew, *my* Matthew, my best friend, my father's step-brother.

My step-uncle.

He was family, the one person that I knew would never let me down. And after my mother died in a wrong place, wrong time kind of thing, I never thought the world would be right again. I was young, so young that as time went on, I started to feel like I would be okay, that things would get better.

So I'd focused on school, knowing that she'd want me to focus on what made me happy.

And I don't know when it had changed, when my feelings for Matthew had started changing from adoration and admiration to ... desire.

It was wrong, a sin, right? He was family, and although not a blood relative, I'd only ever known him as Uncle Matthew.

I was eighteen and finishing up my senior year of high school. I had plans, ambitions.

I had a future.

And I should have been happy, excited about it

all, but over the summer something had changed within me. Something had grown, like a branch of a tree that was twisted and barren, reaching for the sun because that's all it knew.

And Matthew was my sun.

He was all I knew.

I'd felt something shift and turn in me, clawing to get out.

Matthew was outside in the garden, his short dark hair slightly damp at his temples from perspiration. He was installing a new walkway, not something we especially needed, but Matthew liked to stay busy. He liked to work with his hands.

The way his biceps flexed as he worked on the cobblestone had my heart racing. The sight of his tattoo-covered flesh had my body reacting in ways I'd only ever felt with him.

His white T-shirt had smudges of dirt on it, wet from sweat, the sun beating down on him.

My sun.

I was drawn to him like a moth to a flame, my ultimate death awaiting.

He lifted his arm and wiped the sweat from his forehead, his bicep flexing. He was muscular. Having worked in construction most of his adult life had made his body powerful, like a tank.

My hands started aching and I looked down to see my fingers twisted together in my shirt almost violently. I loosened my hold, breathing out slowly, and lifted my head to look back out the window, only to see Matthew looking at me. The air left me viciously and I should have glanced away, but I found myself transfixed at the sight of him, at how he drew out this reaction from me.

Time had no meaning in that moment, no physical hold on me.

I felt a tightness claim me instantly when I saw Mara, our very attractive, very available next-door neighbor walk up to Matthew with a bottle of water in her hand and a come-fuck-me smile plastered on her face.

"Earth to Ivy."

I blinked a few times and pulled my focus away from the window. My cheeks felt hot, the very real possibility that Georgia had seen me watching Matthew embarrassing me.

"I'm here." I cleared my throat and walked back to the table, sitting down across from her. We were in the last month of high school, our senior year, and I couldn't focus.

I hadn't been able to for months now, ever since I

realized what I'd been feeling for Matthew was most definitely not appropriate.

I brought my pencil up to my mouth and started chewing on the end as I zoned out. I could hear Georgia talking, but I wasn't focused on what she said.

I didn't know how long I sat there, but I soon heard the side door open and my heart jumped into my throat. I knew it was Matthew coming inside.

Acting like I had my shit together in that moment was easier said than done, especially seeing as I felt flushed and aroused.

I straightened and looked out toward the hallway, watching as Matthew came into view. He pulled a rag out of his pocket and started wiping the sweat from his forehead, then dragged it down and over the back of his neck.

My fingers were wrapped tightly around the pencil, so hard that it was almost a little painful. He glanced over at us and grinned, giving me a wink and making butterflies move wildly in my stomach, sucking the very air from my lungs.

He stepped into the entryway and leaned against the doorframe, crossing his big, muscular arms over his chest. "You girls studying hard?"

He glanced between Georgia and me and I

cleared my throat, hoping he couldn't see how affected I was by his presence.

"Hardly studying is more like it." Georgia giggled and I glanced over at her, seeing this dreamy-eyed expression on her face.

But I couldn't blame her for being attracted to Matthew. He was all man and I'd fallen down that rabbit hole, too.

He gave me one last look, the corner of his mouth kicking up in a smirk, before the sound of my dad calling for him rang out.

"See ya later, girls," he said and walked away. I couldn't help but sigh at the way his powerful body moved so stealthily.

"Good God. Your uncle is hot as hell," Georgia said.

I glanced over at her and saw her fanning her face, her cheeks pink. Her gaze was locked on mine and she grinned before shrugging.

"He's too old for us, Georgia," I muttered and then realized what I'd said. I glanced up, feeling my eyes widen, but thankfully she hadn't heard the slip in my comment. I should have said he was too old for *her*. I most definitely shouldn't have said he was too old for *us*.

"What can I say? He's every girl's fantasy."

I shook my head and glanced away, hoping she didn't see how much this conversation affected me. I didn't want my secret to come out, definitely not like this.

Lusting after my uncle? Related or not, he'd been in my life for, well, ever. And no doubt people would see my feelings as wrong and sick, taboo.

Maybe I shouldn't care what people thought. But the very idea of Matthew thinking those things was painful. So keeping this to myself, taking it to my grave, was for the best.

ABOUT THE AUTHOR

Want to read more by Jenika Snow? Find all her titles here:

http://jenikasnow.com/bookshelf/

Find the author at:

Newsletter: http://bit.ly/2dkihXD

www.JenikaSnow.com
Jenika_Snow@yahoo.com

Printed in Dunstable, United Kingdom

63400047R00111